A novel by
William Rotsler

Based on the screenplay by
Ken Finkleman

WANDERER BOOKS
Published by Simon & Schuster, New York

This Book is Published by Wanderer Books, a Simon & Schuster Division of
Gulf & Western Corporation Under Exclusive License from Paramount Pictures
Corporation, the Trademark Owner.

All rights reserved
including the right of reproduction
in whole or in part in any form
Published by WANDERER BOOKS
A Simon & Schuster Division of Gulf & Western Corporation
Simon & Schuster Building
1230 Avenue of the Americas
New York, New York 10020
WANDERER and colophon are trademarks of Simon & Schuster
Designed by Ginger Giles
Manufactured in the United States of America
10 9 8 7 6 5 4 3 2
Library of Congress Cataloging in Publication Data
ISBN: 0-671-45576-1

Rotsler, William.
Grease 2.

Summary: The antics of the Pink Ladies, Thunderbirds,
and other members of the new generation at Rydell High.
Sequel to Grease.
[1. School stories] I. Finkleman, Ken. II. Grease 2
(Motion Picture) III. Title.
PZ7.R753Gr [Fic] 82-4800
ISBN 0-671-45576-1 AACR2

☆CHAPTER 1 ☆

The American flag fluttered briskly in the early autumn breeze as it left the experienced hands of Principal McGee. It sent soft "whap-whap" sounds against the brick walls of Rydell High School.

The raising of the flag was a tradition, and one the principal reserved to herself, though disguising her feeling of affection for Old Glory with her usual efficient wryness. She hardly noticed the few leaves skittering along the dew-damp concrete around her ankles.

But the edges of the leaves tickled Blanche Hodel's ankles and, even as she saluted in what she imagined to be military and patriotic perfection, she giggled.

Then came the noise, and Blanche's eyes widened with terror. It sounded every fall and it came every morning, departed every afternoon, and lasted until early summer. It was the sound of screeching tires and the roar of souped-up engines.

Despite herself, Principal McGee gasped. Her hands flew up to her mouth. She couldn't help it. The roar came from every direction, from up and down the street. It was the deep-throated proud thunder of arriving students. The ear-splitting noise came like a surf, irresistible and powerful, charging straight at them.

Then the sight was obliterated by a red and white veil, which limply folded down over them. "Don't let it touch the ground!" Principal McGee snapped, bringing herself out of the paralyzing fear.

Blanche, sputtering and wide-eyed, grasped at the collapsing flag. She and her boss lifted it in time to see the cars screech to a halt. There was a single final unifying roar, and the engines died. Then came the charge.

"Back to school again," groaned one leather-clad youth as he jumped up on his seat.

"Hey, man, I've been havin' a vacation in the sun," his denim-dressed companion said, also jumping lithely from the car. He leered at his friend. "Gettin' lots of *fun* . . . ."

His buddy pointed at him. "Scorin', scorin', scorin' . . . till *now*," he groaned.

The other students, male and female, hopped out of the cars in sweaters and blouses, denim and leather, with strings of pearls and new patches on their jackets.

"*Suddenly*, it's the first day of school again," a snub-nosed blonde said dramatically. She ran up on the wet sidewalk and grabbed at her best friend. "All summer I was *free*!"

A youth with his dark hair greased back in a D.A. hairdo stuck his face between them and leered maniacally. "Well, isn't that just too bad—the board of education strikes again!"

"I gotta start back," a hulking young brute protested. "If I wanna play pro, I gotta play *this* first!"

The buses began arriving, hissing and thumping to a stop. The doors folded open and out came more of Rydell's student body.

Eugene, the class bookworm, was jostled by what appeared to be an ape in a varsity sweater, and his books erupted from his arms, crashing to the damp asphalt in a heap. Appalled at such treatment of books—which he secretly thought of as only slightly less awful than knocking over little old ladies—he knelt to pick them up.

But the next five students that came out

of the bus were like bucking broncos at a rodeo. They stampeded by, knocking him down again. "Hey, man," the first one said, stepping on a history book. "You won't find me till the clock strikes three," he said, pointing a thick finger at the brick buildings. "I'm gonna be *there* till then." He shivered as if it had been a sentence of death.

Eugene huddled over his books protectively, his heart sick at the thought of the broken spine of his history book. Maybe he could rig a splint. . . .

Another car squealed into the last remaining parking place, and a few greased heads turned with delighted smiles. "Hey, the Pink Ladies," one of the jocks said.

The first things out of the car owned and operated by the outlaw sorority were the long and lovely legs of Paulette Rebcheck. She put them out and climbed on top of them, seeming to ignore everyone's stare. She helped Rhonda Ritter out, and briefly took Sharon Cooper's books while her friend got out of the back seat. But she ignored her own little sister, Dolores, who scrambled out after the older and more assured young women.

"Do I havta go back?" Paulette asked the world at large, fluffing her blonde hair and giving the school a scowl.

"Yeah. . . ." Rhonda sighed.

"Back to school again," Sharon added, thinking of the faded pleasures of summer and how good she looked in her daring new bikini.

"Oh, look," Dolores said. "There's Steph."

The jocks on the lawn backed up, jostling Eugene again. Their grins were wide as they gave Stephanie Zinone room to walk on her route to join the rest of the Pink Ladies.

"Whoa," one said, leering.

The leader of the sorority winked but kept right on moving, assured in her stride.

"Hey, troops—hold it!" another jock sighed, watching the rear view of the blonde and beautiful Miss Zinone.

The Pink Ladies left their car and crossed the sidewalk to climb on the benches that surrounded the flagpole. Other students stopped and watched the antics of their principal and her assistant trying to get the flag raised.

Sharon sniffed the autumn air. "She's late again!" she said with exaggerated aloofness. *"Personally,* I think that being late demonstrates terrible leadership qualities."

Then Rhonda spotted Stephanie pushing her way through the students. "Here she comes!"

Stephanie broke through and gestured with her shoulder. "Ladies, let's go!"

They hopped down and pushed back through the crowd of incoming students. From all around them they heard the usual complaints spoken at the beginning of the fall semester.

"History and math," groaned one. "It's just a pain in the—"

"Chemistry and history destroys the human brain," agreed another who had been getting D's for two years.

"Don't they know I have better things to do?" a bouffant-haired young girl grumbled. "I'm too busy for this."

The jock next to her puffed out his chest. "Hey, sweetstuff, am I one of the better things?" She gave him the most punishing of looks and moved on.

"Well, it's that time again," an athlete said.

"But *why*?" the other jock asked.

"'Cause you need to graduate if you ever want to play the pros, that's why, Galen."

"Oh . . . oh, yeah."

"Uh-oh, the coach," a jock muttered.

Coach Calhoun jogged up to the school entrance, his gray sweat suit stained, carrying a basketball under his arm like a football. He was panting and gasping for air and didn't seem to notice the purse-sized dog bit-ing his pants leg with grim determination.

The sharp-nosed, bushy-eyebrowed coach tossed the basketball in the general direction of the athletes he had spotted. "Okay, you lunks, it's bye-bye fun."

The basketball bounced and one of the young men caught it and immediately passed it to a taller companion. "Get your homework done," the coach yelled after them. "And you better be in by ten!" he added. He lost more good players to poor grades and sexy seventeen-year-olds than to anything else, he thought gloomily. If I were designing school systems, he thought, you'd have to qualify in at least one sport before you could go to class and graduate only if your runs batted in or slam-dunks were good enough.

Coach Calhoun grunted as he veered around a group of pink-clad female students practicing cheerleading. If my boys kept their eyes on the ball instead of the bouncing cheerleaders, he thought, I'd win more games.

"Ohhh . . . I guess I *gotta* take these classes," Sharon said.

"Back to good ol' Rydell," Paulette muttered.

"Ladies," Stephanie said, "let's face it . . . we gotta go back." Mutual groans and muttered complaints came from the girls.

"Sigh," sighed Paulette.

"Triple sigh," breathed Sharon.

Principal McGee was tying off the flag rope when another sound came, the deeper, nastier sound—the one she dreaded above all others. She turned her head as Blanche gasped.

Three motorcycles, one with a sidecar, came down the street, weaving back and forth. They crashed over the curb, chewed their way across the school lawn, running down a neatly lettered little sign, which said KEEP OFF THE GRASS, and swung to a roaring stop at the sidewalk, almost running over the Pink Ladies.

"The T-birds," a jock sneered quietly.

"The T-birds," a freshman girl sighed.

Leather-gloved thumbs shoved at goggles and one by one their faces were revealed. Goose McKenzie—the tallest—dark, curly hair and a grin. Lou Dimucci—his eyes wise, his dark hair combed back in the required D.A. shape, the T-bird name and symbol across the back of his black leather jacket. Davey Jaworski—the smallest—his leather collar turned up in imitation of all the rest in the very epitome of cool. And last—but far from least—their undisputed leader, Johnny Nogerilli.

Johnny was the handsomest, his zippered black leather jacket, the sharpest, his

14

oiled hair, the best-shaped, his swagger, the most insolent. And he knew it.

The T-birds were the power in the school and were not reluctant to prove it: It was a tradition that had gone back for years. The T-birds were *it* and you better believe it. They had tradition, they had clout, they had numbers, they had class, but most of all, they were cool.

It wasn't just the dark shades, the tight denims, the black leathers, the boots, and the cigarettes that they had learned to dangle at just the right angle. It wasn't the sexy swagger, the come-backs and put-ons, or the insults. It wasn't just that they were trend-setters, muscle, or rule-breakers. It was *all* of those things together—a smooth, seamless, perfect case of collective cool.

The T-birds were cool, man.

And don't you *ever* doubt it.

Jaworski opened his eyes wide in mock horror, and the rest of the T-birds grinned derisively. Coming up the sidewalk were three of the Preptones, neat and groomed in their school sweaters, slacks pressed, bucks buffed, shirts buttoned, their crew cuts exactly the same. They snapped their fingers in rhythm, and their steps were light. They hummed faintly to themselves, lost in some well-practiced song, dreaming of "National Bandstand" and a record contract.

The T-birds looked at three-fourths of the quartet in disbelief. Could *anyone* actually be *that* square? "Cute," Jaworski muttered.

They all dismounted and adjusted their duds before strutting down the center walk. Lou Dimucci grunted with disgust. "Senior year." He shrugged with resignation. "The home stretch."

Davey spread his hand in the air. "My old man wants me to go to junior college after grad. What're you gonna do, Johnny?"

The leader of the T-birds, the coolest of the cool, said just one word. "Sleep."

Davey persisted. "No, I mean what're you guys gonna be when you grow up?"

"A burden on society," Goose McKenzie said, bringing grins to the faces of his friends.

Their grins widened as they saw Miss Mason, the music and English teacher, coming up from the faculty parking lot. They stopped to watch, fascinated by the woman. Yvette Mason was the youngest member of the Rydell faculty and self-consciously, the prettiest. She stopped, felt her hair, then pulled a can of hairspray from her purse. With a practiced gesture she encased her head in a mist, but the can sputtered empty before she had satisfactorily sealed her head from the environment. Deftly, she tossed the can into a trash can. While the empty can was still in the air, she lifted another from her purse and put on the final layer. She then continued to walk toward the classrooms.

"Hello, Miss Mason," a sorority girl said, trotting past.

"Hello, girls," the teacher smiled, her eyes crinkling into slits.

"I love your hair, Miss Mason," a second girl said, trotting by.

"Why, thank you," the teacher said, dropping the can back into her purse and patting her blonde locks.

The sorority girl caught up to her friend and whispered, "All three hundred platinum pounds of it!" They cracked up, gripping each other's arms and shouldering through the door.

The T-birds hoisted themselves onto the sidewalk railing that led the final yards to the school buildings. Johnny snapped his fingers and Davey fished out a pack of cigarettes. They all lit up.

Hooking their boots under the lower rail they sat with shoulders slumped and oogled the passing girls, especially the new and curious freshman females. From time to time they made kissing sounds at the more delectable ones, and, from time to time, received a glare from an older student who

17

had been the victim of their pranks in the past.

Then Yvette Mason came up the walk. They saw her pat her hair, frown, and stop long enough to pluck the can of hairspray from her purse and resume spraying.

"Hello, Miss Mason," they all said in unison.

She stopped spraying long enough to look at them sternly. "I'd like to see all of you in music appreciation this year." They just grinned at her. She seemed to discover the can of spray in her hand and gave herself a small final burst as she continued her walk. The T-birds drooled after her, exaggerating their reactions.

Nogerilli said, "I'd like to see all of *you* in music appreciation this year."

"I think I'm in love," Davey said, clutching at his heart. Johnny Nogerilli slapped him on the arm.

They were all watching Miss Mason's retreat and did not see the approach of chubby little Bruce Sanders, almost invisible under the black bulk of a double bass. The lad staggered and the tip of the bass swung by Davey's nose. The T-bird ducked back, lost his balance, and started falling. He clutched at the T-birds on either side, and all four went over in a tangle of arms, legs, and heavy boots.

The students trooped on by, ignoring the writhing mass of T-birds suddenly made very uncool. Further along, the Pink Ladies, with Dolores in attendance, were raising their hands.

Together they said, "The Pink Ladies' pledge: to act cool, to look cool, and to be cool. Till death do us part—*think pink!*"

They reassembled their proud faces into a "cool" expression and set off toward the future, which happened to be somewhere inside the brick buildings.

To recapture their cool, the T-birds had transformed the dumping onto the grass into a leg-wrestling contest. Then their ears sent a warning to their brains: motorcycles were nearby.

The Cycle Lords drove by, and with various gestures of fingers and forearms saluted the grass-stained T-birds. The T-birds scrambled to their feet and looked around for something to be cool about. They selected Bruce Sanders, still struggling with his double bass, which was about forty pounds too heavy for him.

Goose grabbed the bass and Nogerilli grabbed Bruce and they carried their captives to the flagpole. It took only a moment to tie the flag rope to the neck of the bass and start it skyward. Bruce wriggled free as all the T-birds began to salute the ascending

19

musical instrument. He jumped for the bass but missed.

Goose tied off the rope in a complex knot and cinched it tight. Then they wheeled and sauntered off, the coolest of the cool, lords of all they surveyed, the dudes no one messed with.

"Comb," Nogerilli said, holding out his hand.

Lou slapped a comb into his hand, imitating a surgical nurse, and Johnny combed his hair in sweeping gestures, patting it into place just right.

"Door," Johnny said.

Davey jumped ahead and opened the heavy school door. But before Johnny Nogerilli could walk through, the Pink Ladies stepped in, hips swinging, and sauntered through with lifted noses. The T-birds just grinned and projected imagined movies in which selected members of the Pink Ladies starred in their fantasies.

Johnny looked up at the Rydell High School sign and sighed. "Gentlemen, start your engines." They went inside.

The bass still swung slowly in the wind.

☆CHAPTER 2☆

Frenchy Lefevre grinned up at the tall
young Englishman, her dark hair ruffled by
the autumn breeze. "When your cousin
Sandy told me you were coming to school in
America, I said, 'Sandy, any cousin of yours
is a cousin of mine.'"

Michael Carrington smiled. "Sandy said
you're the one who knows the ropes around
Rydell."

"The ropes are my specialty," Frenchy
said. "See, I spent two years here at Rydell
before dropping out to go to beauty school
where I flunked tinting when my hair turned
pink." She shrugged and made a gesture.
"So I switched to skin care."

"Tinting is out, skin care is in," Michael
said.

"Right. That's why I'm back at Rydell, to

21

get my chemistry so I can mix my own cosmetics."

"Makes sense," the British youth nodded.

Their heads went up at the sound of the bell. "Hurry up," Frenchy said, hugging her books and starting off. "You're gonna love Rydell."

They trotted up the steps and into the building.

The halls were jammed with kids in the standard confusion of first days. "They moved my home room," one passing student complained.

"I got algebra the *first thing* in the morning," groaned a girl.

"Latin is all Greek to me," griped a boy. "It was Greek last year and it'll be Greek again this year."

"Did you see that freshman chick with the chest?" a sophomore asked his friend.

"I've got my locker only two down from Stephanie Zinone's," the other said happily.

"Forget her, dumbo, you got about as much chance with her as an East German has getting over that new wall they're putting up."

"Have you seen 'El Cid'?" Elayne Miller asked her best friend. "That Heston is just so *dreamy.* I mean, for an older man."

Marji Ackerman said with a sigh, "So's President Kennedy."

They stopped at their lockers after checking the numbers. They opened them up and stuck in their books, chatting as they taped pictures to the inside of the door. A grinning James Garner in his black Bret Maverick hat. Blond, smiling Troy Donahue from "Surfside 6." Glowering Ben Casey. Paul Anka, Paul Newman, Pat Boone, Frankie Avalon. Chubby Checker with his hips in a strange position. Dick Van Dyke, Elizabeth Taylor, Peter Nero in a tuxedo, Jack Paar with a panda. Bob Stack with a machine gun, Eric Fleming and that skinny kid Eastwood with six-guns, dreamy Richard Chamberlain in a surgical gown, Kooky Byrnes with a comb.

A few lockers down, Rhonda Ritter was looking at herself in the mirror she had hung in her locker. "From the front this is a perfect nose." She turned her head and her mouth turned down as she stared at herself almost with disgust. "From the side this nose does not belong on this face."

Stephanie pulled her head out of her locker to say, "Then dump the nose and hold the face."

Paulette Rebcheck shut her locker and put on the combination lock, which was set to the same setting as Maynard Krebs's locker number: 0000. She looked at Sharon Cooper standing next to her, looking at herself critically in a purse mirror. "What's the new look, Sharon?"

"Jackie Kennedy," the girl answered at once. "It *only* landed her a president."

"Yeah, well," Paulette responded. "*Movie Confessions* says JFK secretly prefers the Marilyn Monroe look."

Sharon sniffed and continued her minute examination. Paulette's attention was drawn to the sight of black leather in the hall. She saw Johnny Nogerilli and Goose McKenzie moving languidly through the crowded hall. She noticed Johnny had a cigarette cupped in his hand. He took a surreptitious drag, glancing her way only casually.

"Hi, Johnny," she said excitedly, her cool definitely slipping.

Nogerilli hardly acknowledged her existence, giving her only a terse nod before his eyes found Stephanie and locked. He stopped and, letting the chattering crowd ebb around him, watched Stephanie pull a greasy jacket from her bag and hang it up in the back of her locker. His eyes took in the freshly taped photos and clippings on her inner door—Johnny Cash in black, Tony Eisely in a Hawaiian shirt, Roger Smith under the "77 Sunset Strip" sign, Audrey

Hepburn in a bathtub made into a couch from "Breakfast at Tiffany's."

"I really like your hair in the back," Paulette said. "Really cool, Johnny."

Johnny held out his hand toward Goose, his eyes still on Stephanie who was still stacking things into her locker. "Thanks," he said. "Comb," he commanded. Goose slapped a comb into his hand.

While Nogerilli combed his D.A. with slow, loving gestures, and tried to think of how to open a conversation with Stephanie, Goose reached past the blonde and pulled out the sleeve of her jacket, holding it to one side to see the crest woven into the back panel. It read JAKE'S SERVICE STATION.

"I see you're still working at your old man's service station," he said.

"Stuff it, Goose," Stephanie said at once.

Nogerilli gave Goose the comb back and leaned close to the attractive girl, whispering confidentially in her ear as he rested a hand on the lockers, "Yeah, what's the story?" As Goose started to get closer, Nogerilli shoved him back.

"You know the story, Johnny," Stephanie said, reaching in to add a paperback to her books on the shelf. "It's over."

Nogerilli frowned. "Yeah, well, that ain't good enough."

Stephanie's blue eyes turned to stare

25

into Nogerilli's dark ones. "Let's not have a scene, okay, Johnny?"

The leather-jacketed gang leader whispered assertively, "There's no scene!" He seemed appalled that there was any suggestion of uncoolness.

Nogerilli started to speak again, but saw Davey and Dimucci approaching. "Hey, Johnny," Davey said, grinning.

"What's the scene?" Dimucci asked.

Nogerilli turned on them angrily. "There's no scene! All right?"

Baffled, both Davey and Dimucci stepped back. "Sorreeee," they said in unison.

Sharon dropped her mirror into her purse and closed it with a snap. "Hi, Louis," she said to Dimucci.

"Lou to you," he frowned, feeling a little uncomfortable. Women were supposed to keep quiet, keep cool, and let the guys do all the advances.

Goose snooped around during the awkward silence and peeked into Rhonda's locker. The inside of the door and large sections of the interior walls were covered with photos, clippings, and posters of Vince Fontaine, the host of "National Bandstand." "Hey, what's this, the Vince Fontaine National Library?"

"Quiet, *pleeeze*," Davey and Dimucci said together.

Rhonda glared at them. "Laugh, you jerks, but just wait until I turn up on 'National Bandstand'!"

Goose snorted. "Maybe you'll turn *up* on 'National Bandstand' but your nose'll still be turnin' *down*, Rhonda."

The T-birds laughed, and Nogerilli joined in, glad for an honorable way to detach himself from Stephanie. Things were *not* going as he had hoped and planned. Fight again another day. Think it out. Make plans. But stay cool.

He gathered his friends together with a gesture and they continued down the hall. Rhonda glared after them, then took out her mirror again. "I gotta do it," she muttered. "The nose goes. 'Bandstand,' here I come."

"If I were you, Rhonda," Paulette said, "I wouldn't fool around with Mother Nature."

Rhonda sniffed. "You've fooled around with everyone else, Paulette." They walked down the hall toward class with Sharon following. Stephanie closed her locker, clicked on her combination lock, then followed. She didn't see the class bookworm, Eugene, coming down the hall with tall, good-looking Michael Carrington.

Michael had his arms full: notebooks, schedules, extra pencils, a combination lock, a couple of school books he had been told he'd need, and a couple of photographs of home. He was also suppressing a smile at the way Eugene was talking to him—loudly and slowly—as if he was a foreigner who did not speak English at all.

"How long have you been in America?" Eugene asked.

Michael said, "Just about a week. I'm staying with my aunt and uncle."

Eugene pointed with his arm fully extended. "There are the lockers. Take any locker that doesn't have a lock on it. They steal every . . ."

Then he saw the T-birds, who had seen him pointing at their section of lockers. Without finishing his sentence, Eugene spun around and walked away quickly with visions of mayhem in his head. But Michael had not seen Eugene's quick reversal. He stopped before a section of somewhat battered lockers and hooked one open with a finger extended from beneath his load. He saw but gave no significance to the big "T" scratched into the paint on the door.

He turned to thank Eugene. "Thanks, I . . ." No Eugene. He looked around, puzzled.

The locker door was slammed shut with

a resounding clang, and Michael's books were knocked out of his hands. Paper and pencils started to slip away.

Michael found himself looking into the glowering face of a leather-jacketed T-bird. Davey Jaworski snarled, "What do you think you're doing?"

"Hi," Michael said, blinking. Americans were known to be rough and tough, but he thought this was going too far. "I was just putting a few things in my locker."

"*His* locker," three of the gang said at once. "Well, excuse *us*."

"Yes," Michael said, turning toward the locker, "I . . ."

Suddenly, a hand seized his shoulder and swung the young Briton around. Michael found himself staring into the angry face of Nogerilli.

"No one touches these lockers, friend. Or can't you read?" Michael followed his stiffly pointed finger to the big "T" carved in the locker door. Nogerilli's gesture included four more doors, all of them emblazoned with large T's. One of them had "T-birds" added. "That," Johnny Nogerilli said, "spells T-bird."

"Which spells *us*," Goose growled.

Nogerilli opened the locker that Michael had opened. "And this is a sacred and pro-tected landmark."

"A slice of American history," Dimucci said belligerently.

"You dig?" Nogerilli asked. He opened the door dramatically and pointed at what he knew would still be there, even after summer vacation and the lack of a lock. The locker was almost a memorial, with photos of previous T-bird groups, a 1956 license plate, captured Cycle Lord colors, a pair of lacy panties with four stars added in black ink, pictures of Robert Conrad, "The Untouchables," the guys from "Route 66," Jimmy Cagney, Bogart, James Arness, and Richard Boone in his Paladin gear.

Michael nodded, "I think I understand." It was a shrine to obscure standards and goals that he barely understood.

"Good," Nogerilli said.

"My name's Michael Carrington."

Goose's eyebrows went up at the English accent. "And I'm the Duke of Earl."

Nogerilli opened the door of a nearby locker. "And here's *your* locker!"

Violently, all four of the T-birds grabbed Michael and shoved him into the open locker. What had been left in Michael's grasp was dumped onto the floor. The slamming door struck him painfully on the elbow.

The T-birds dusted off their hands theatrically and then swaggered off, triumphant in an easy four-to-one victory. "A perfect fit," Nogerilli said, and they all laughed.

Michael shouldered open the locker with a crash and squeezed out, rubbing his elbow and taking a quick inventory of his bruises. He looked up to see a remarkably pretty girl bending over to help gather up his spilled papers and books. She straightened up and gave them to him solemnly.

"You okay?" Stephanie asked.

He stared into her blue eyes, saw the parted pink lips, the long gleaming blonde hair, the perfect skin. "Uh . . . yeah . . . fine. Thanks."

Stephanie looked down the corridor at the leather backs disappearing around a corner. "Don't let those jerks bug you." She said it absently, as much to herself as the young Englishman.

Michael roused himself from his rude staring. "Uh . . . I won't. Don't worry. Thanks. I . . ."

But the blonde vision was walking away.

☆CHAPTER 3☆

Stephanie walked into Yvette Mason's English class very much aware that Johnny Nogerilli was close behind her. And that klutz, Goose, behind him. She saw Miss Mason writing her name on the blackboard, then turned to confront Johnny and his henchman.

"When are you guys gonna grow up?" she asked with obvious disgust in her voice.

"The nerd invaded our sacred turf," Goose complained.

Nogerilli was not about to be deterred from his intended idea. "I want to talk to you," he said intently to Stephanie, unable to keep his usual tone of menace out of his voice. "Meet me for a smoke after class."

"I quit," the young blonde said. "It's bad for your health." She turned away and found a seat. Nogerilli sat next to her, and Goose, after pushing away a kid with glasses, sat behind them.

"And standin' me up is also bad for your health," Nogerilli continued.

Stephanie looked flatly at him. "Says who?"

"Says the sturgeon general of the United States, Stephanie," Goose grinned.

Miss Mason turned away from the blackboard. "Everyone, please take a seat," she called out.

Goose grabbed a passing girl's rear end. "I got mine," he announced. The senior girl spun around and slugged him with her fist. Goose looked surprised and angry, then started to rise, but the desk arm trapped him and he swung at her ineffectually. Others in the class started yelling encouragement to the girl. In an instant, the class was in chaos.

Miss Mason rapped on her desk with a ruler, crying, "Order! Order!"

The only one to hear her was Billy Warren, who yelled out, "A ham and cheese with fries to go!"

The class broke up laughing and the offended girl flounced up to her seat as Michael Carrington slipped quietly into the room. He took a seat next to Stephanie, with Nogerilli on the other side of her. Stephanie looked at him and he smiled, but she didn't respond.

Michael shrugged inwardly as Miss Mason slowly brought the class to attention. American girls, he decided, were not any different than British girls—they were *all* hard to understand.

Blanche Hodel was tacking sheets of mimeographed paper to an office bulletin board—schedules, dress codes, home room teachers, changes in classes, fire department notices, civilian defense announcements.

Principal McGee sat at her desk, the microphone to the loudspeaker system before her and her eyes on the big clock. "The chimes, Blanche," she said.

Blanche looked at her watch. "It's almost nine."

"Not the *time*," the woman principal said. "The *chimes*!"

"Oh!" Blanche dumped her papers on a desk and lumbered toward the little set of brass chimes. She grabbed the mallet and hammered away violently and noisily, stopping only when Miss McGee grabbed her arm.

"Good morning, Rydell, and welcome one and all to a new school year," she said into the microphone in her usually cheery public voice.

In Miss Mason's class, everyone had stopped at the sound of the chimes and listened, more or less. "I know this is going to be an exciting and stimulating year for all," Principal McGee said cheerfully.

Bruce Sanders watched with widening eyes as Goose McKenzie pulled out a switchblade. Goose stared threateningly at Bruce, then flicked the blade open in a theatrical gesture. He began to carve his initials into the chairarm. He did it slowly, deliberately, trying to think out how he should do it. "GM" or "GMK"? Or "EMK" for his real name? Or "Goose"? Feeling the hardness of the wood, he decided on "GM."

They were also listening in Wally Spears's biology class. The bland, bespectacled teacher sat at his desk, his name written across the blackboard behind him, shaking nervously. He swallowed again, then again. Nervously, he shook a pill from a plastic jar, picked up a glass of water, and gulped most of it down quickly.

"First," said Principal McGee's voice from the loudspeaker over the door, "I'd like to extend a special welcome back to our own Mister Spears who made a miraculous recovery from the mental exhaustion that sent him to the hospital last spring."

At the sound of his name, Spears blinked, swallowed, grinned nervously for a full second, then reached for another pill.

At the back of the room, during McGee's announcement, Lou Dimucci reached into a wire cage and caught a trembling white mouse. He passed it to Davey, who dropped it onto the desk of Beverly Beachwood, who was sleeping peacefully with her mouth open.

"Welcome back, Mister Spears," the principal continued. "We're all rooting for you."

At the word "rooting," several things happened at once. The mouse sniffed its way toward the open mouth. Dimucci and Jaworski leaned closer to watch the reaction. Beverly opened her eyes, stared sleepily at the nearby faces, two blurs in the distance and a white blur right in front of her. Then she focused on the white blur.

Her blood-curdling scream reminded Davey of Hazel Court in "Dr. Blood's Coffin." Mr. Spears's second pill and glass of water went flying off the desk. And the mouse scuttled onto the floor and disappeared. Principal McGee's voice droned on.

"Rydell is very proud of her extra-curricular activities. Please come out for band tryouts. If you play an instrument it's much better to play with a group than with yourself."

Davey Jaworski guffawed, and Beverly Beachwood stopped yowling to show a trembling grin.

In the chemistry lab, Frenchy Lefevre stood next to Joyce Massoglia, who was wearing a beauty salon smock and a patient expression. Frenchy was applying a facial cream from a brew that was simmering over a burner, with a concoction from a maze of tubes and retorts dripping into it.

"Also," added the principal over the raspy speakers, "tryouts for the annual Rydell talent show will begin next month."

Frenchy absently turned up the burner under her secret concoction and went back to dabbing on blobs of the gooey mess. The girls were only half-listening to their principal drone on about shifted classes and new hall-pass rules when the beaker exploded.

The room was filled with smoke, and droplets of the greenish goo were stuck to the ceiling. "Gee," said Frenchy from her seat on the floor, "I'm beginning to wonder if Madame Curie went through troubles like this to make *her* great discovery. What do you think, Joyce? Joyce? *Joyce?*"

Frenchy put her chin in her hand.

"Darn. That's the second volunteer I've lost. You'd think they'd be proud to be part of a great discovery. . . ."

In Yvette Mason's English class, Johnny Nogerilli was stretching out a wad of pink gum as far as he could. His record had been set in science class two years before and stood at nearly thirty inches, a full arm's length.

Stephanie Zinone was reading the September *Road & Track*. Paulette was reading a copy of *Life* with Marilyn Monroe on the cover. Goose McKenzie was playing solitaire on his desk and cheating while quietly humming Sam Cooke's "Chain Gang." Bruce Sanders was wondering why they had shifted "The Adventures of Ozzie and Harriet" to Thursday night. Just what *did* Ozzie do for a living?

"Come out and show us your talent," Principal McGee said. "*You* could win the grand prize."

Johnny Nogerilli thought about the prize that was Stephanie Zinone. Michael Carrington thought about her as well, but in a different way. To him she was not a prize, but a possible . . . a possible *what*? Girlfriend?

"Also, as part of Rydell's student exchange program we are fortunate to have a straight A student . . ."

Michael Carrington's attention snapped back to reality and he felt eyes upon him. He saw that Miss Mason had written his name on the blackboard.

". . . all the way from England, by the name of Michael Carrington," the principal said. "Let's show him that old Rydell hospitality."

Everyone was looking at him. Even the blonde with the big blue eyes.

"Now let's all have a wonderful year," concluded the principal. There was a rustling noise, then they heard her say, "Shut if *off*, Blanche. There's a—"

A stretch of silence that embarrassed the young Briton followed. Then Miss Mason smiled and said, "Stand up, Michael, please." He stood up, on the verge of blushing. "Say hello to Michael Carrington," Yvette Mason said.

"Hello to Michael Carrington," the entire class said in a super-sweet voice. All except the blonde, Michael noted. She didn't seem to respond at all.

Michael sat down, aware of the stares. "Straight A's, huh?" Nogerilli grunted. He laughed and made sucking sounds, and several of the others joined in, but Michael ignored them. He opened a book and stared blankly at the page.

He had guessed that America was going

to be . . . different. Not this rough, though. The Americans he had met in Great Britain had all been open, happy, easy to know, easy to like, even if they had seemed a bit gauche and brash. But friendly, always friendly. Britons were too stuffy, he thought, too proper, too concerned about appearances.

Yes, the States and the Americans were okay, he thought. But he just wondered if he could fit in.

☆CHAPTER 4☆

Even after a week of practice, the marching band was still making a backward "E" in "Rydell" two out of three times.

The sorority girls seated in the stands saw the cute English boy, Carrington, come out in his gym gear. Beverly Beachwood waved her hand and called, "Michael!"

He looked up and hesitated as they got up and hurried down toward him. He was often put off by Marji Ackerman, who just wanted to hear his English accent, and by Joyce Massoglia, who had the idea he must know royalty. After all, England was so *tiny*, you know.

Beverly waved at him again as she came down the steps. "We have to talk to you!"

As they came toward him, Michael saw Blanche Hodel climbing down from her ladder, bullhorn in hand. Her voice bellowed out across the football field. "No! Wait! Stop! The 'E' is backwards!" she said. "Fix the 'E'! Fix the 'E'! Next routine! Into the arcs!" She never noticed how close her horn was to a small freshman's ear.

"Tubas are wonderful!" she bellowed. "Trumpets are marvelous! Drums—try to stay on the beat! Remember—you *are* the beat!"

The sorority girls caught up to him and Michael said, "Look, I've got to do some laps. . . ."

"We'll go with you," Beverly said.

"About the talent show, Michael," Joyce Massoglia said.

"I have some classical piano," he said, "but I—"

"Then you *must* help with the talent show auditions," Beverly Beachwood insisted. "I will *not* take No for an answer."

He looked apologetic. "I haven't played in quite a—"

"Beverly has *never* taken No for an answer," Joyce Massoglia said firmly.

Michael shrugged and trotted on, while the sorority girls dropped back. Now what am I getting into? Michael thought. He jogged right past a group of students assembled before Coach Calhoun.

The T-birds were among the athletes

lined up ready to run through a double line of old automobile tires lying on the grass.

The beady-eyed coach bellowed enthusiastically at them. "All right, men, in place, in place. Knees up! Knees up! They're gonna grab for your ankles, that's why you want those knees up, up, *up!* Up, up, up, up!" The athletes dutifully raised their knees higher as they ran in place.

"Now, through the tires. Come on, Tripp, you're first! Come on. Through the tires."

Galen Tripp, a senior, almost danced as he ran, expertly putting a cleated foot in the center of each tire. The ones that followed did not do as well, and the T-birds were the worst.

"Not *on* the tires, *through* the tires!" Calhoun yelled. "That was terrible, terrible." He pointed at the four T-birds. "Okay, you guys go back."

They grumbled and obeyed, knees high, prancing. "Football is like life," Calhoun shouted at them. "You gotta play to win. To win, you gotta play like a team. You gotta eat together, sleep together, work together, *breathe* together. Eat, sleep, work, breathe. Eat, sleep, work, breathe! Eat, sleep, work, breathe!"

The T-birds picked up the chant. "Eat, sleep, work, *breathe!* Eat, *sleep*, work, *breathe! Eat, sleep, work, breathe!"* They chanted heavily. "Eat! Sleep! Work! Breathe!"

Calhoun yelled. "Okay, go get 'em! Go get 'em!"

The T-birds started running through the tires, this time doing much better. "Eat! *Sleep!* Work! *Breathe!"* But they didn't stop after the last tire. They kept on going, charging right into the group of waiting players, attacking them unexpectedly, blocking and hitting heavily.

"Wait!" Calhoun yelled. "Those are our guys!"

But the joys of combat were upon them and the T-birds just crashed happily into jock after jock.

☆ ☆ ☆

The Pink Ladies were strolling. Or trolling, as Sharon sometimes called it— casual, cool, and untouchable. Paulette and Stephanie lagged behind the others. Paulette glanced at her blonde friend, licked her lips, and asked the question casually. "So what's the story with you and Johnny?"

Stephanie shrugged. "Let's just say I outgrew him over the summer."

"Well," her friend said, tossing her short

44

blonde curls, "he sure hasn't lost the hots for you."

Stephanie sighed and it took her a moment to answer. "Johnny just hasn't learned. When you're dead, lie down. Anyway, there's *got* to be more to life than makin' out."

A frown creased Paulette's brow. "You know . . . I never thought of it that way." After a moment's thought, she looked up to see the English guy walking along, surrounded by several of the sorority girls in their neat sweaters and strings of pearls. "Preppy alert!" Paulette cried. "Preppy alert!"

Stephanie grinned. "All male periscopes down!" Sharon and Rhonda laughed and looked back at Stephanie.

But the sorority girls pretended not to have heard them and shepherded Michael past. They looked over the fence as Frenchy Lefevre called out to Michael, but he ignored her, too. They pressed for an answer. *"Well?"* they all asked at once.

Michael pulled away from the girls and nodded. "Okay. Okay, I'll do it." The girls smiled and started whispering among themselves as Michael went over to Frenchy.

"I think he's kinda cute," Beverly said.

"That *accent!*" Marji Ackerman sighed.

Frenchy smiled warmly at the approaching tall young Briton. "How's your first week been, Michael?"

But Michael was staring back at Stephanie as she sauntered along the cement walk. He wasn't really listening as he answered. "Fine," he said politely. "Yours?"

"Great!" she said enthusiastically. "There is *such* a fascinating world of chemistry out there."

"How well do you know Stephanie Zinone?" he asked with his eyes still on the leader of the Pink Ladies.

"Oh, Stephanie is one of my very best . . ." She stopped as she realized who he was staring at. She put her hand on his arm. "Holy cow." She looked nervous, then plunged ahead. "Look, Michael, I think there's something you might not understand. Stephanie's a Pink Lady. Which means if you're not a T-bird—which you are *not*—you can look but you don't touch. I wouldn't even look."

Michael nodded. But even to Frenchy it was obvious that her warning had not sunk in. Holy cow, she thought.

☆ ☆ ☆

Coach Calhoun spoke very calmly to his assembly of young men. "Football isn't just a game. Football is life itself. To get to the top you need teamwork, luck, courage, sensitivity to your fellow men, and, most of all, the killer instinct." The coach frowned. "So when you go for that quarterback, I want you to . . ."

The athletes stared at the coach, then almost jumped as he screamed, *"Kill him!"*

The coach ordered them up against the tackling sled, and the T-birds threw themselves into it, glad for the workout. The big wooden structure with its shoulder pads began to move down the grass, with Coach Calhoun backing up ahead of them.

Nogerilli grunted at Dimucci next to him. "Check *this* out," he said. The T-birds looked through the timbers to see the Cycle Lords cruising down the track, then bumping over the concrete lip to drive defiantly across the worn grass.

All the football players were looking at the Cycle Lords now, but their cleated feet still dug into the grass, and they were still pushing hard as the coach continued his frenzy.

"Mangle an arm! Maim! Kill!"

Then the coach noticed the raw earth of the construction pit where they were putting in the new sprinkler system. "Pit! No! Wait! Stop! Don't maim! Don't kill!"

But it was too late. The tackling sled

47

shoved him right into the ditch. The players didn't even look, but stopped and stood up to witness the confrontation between the two gangs.

Nogerilli and his T-birds watched with expressionless faces as the Cycle Lords cruised noisily, but slowly, right by them.

The rival leader was hard-faced, with his "colors" suitably fierce. "Nogerilli," he said in a flat voice, acknowledging the existence of the T-bird boss.

"Balmudo," Nogerilli responded, just as cool.

The motorcycles continued across the grass, insolently bumping back onto the gravel track and out of the field area.

"Those cockroaches are gonna cross our turf one time too many," muttered Goose.

Dimucci nodded in agreement. "We should take care of them tonight."

For a moment, Nogerilli was silent. The "invasion" was a deliberate provocation, a non-violent gesture of impending violence and the latest in a long line of mutual insults, which they had exchanged for years. Ever since Nogerilli was a punk kid and Danny Zucco was the chief honcho. Time and place, he thought. Time and place. Military precision. You never attack blindly. You *never* fight on the other's terms.

"Tonight we bowl," he said.

Goose looked at Dimucci, who looked at Davey Jaworski, who shrugged. Johnny was the boss, leader and war chief in one, and what Johnny said went. Besides, if you *didn't* do what he said you'd get a fist in your face.

There was a raucous noise. Then the bandleader at the other end of the field held up his baton to the musicians who were tuning their instruments. The "Washington Post March" blasted out across the field.

Nogerilli saw the Pink Ladies come out from between the bleachers followed at a distance by Michael Carrington. He watched them do a quick little parody dance to the marching music, then trot on out. No one at all paid any attention to the muffled sounds of Coach Calhoun, who was still stuck in the construction pit. The band began marching downfield toward them, and Sharon, in the lead, had to shout to be heard.

"Are we bowling tonight?"

"That's right," Nogerilli nodded. He pointed a thick finger at Paulette. "And Paulette—!"

"Yeah, Johnny?" she said breathlessly with her eyes sparkling.

Nogerilli let his gaze slip toward

Stephanie for one quick look, watching for effect as he said, "I want you to look *special!* Dig?"

"*No* problem," Paulette answered, smiling widely.

The Pink Ladies danced back as the band came relentlessly onward, cutting between the T-birds and the Pink Ladies. But in the center stood Michael, with the horns and drums and flutes streaming past him. When the last musician had passed, Michael could see only the backs of the football players as they headed for the showers. He turned and started back, passing Blanche Hodel as she came fluttering onto the field.

She peered down into the pit and in her squeaky voice said, "Mister Calhoun! What on earth are you doing down there?"

Calhoun put up his hand and made an incoherent growling sound, attempting to scale the steep, crumbling sides. Blanche bent over and grabbed his extended hand, but her left shoe stepped hard on Calhoun's other hand.

"Your foot, Blanche," Calhoun said in a tight voice.

"Oh!" She jumped back off his hand and released the hand in her grasp. Calhoun tumbled back into the pit. Blanche poised on the edge with her hand to her mouth in shock. "Oh! I'm very sorry, I'm so—"

Bump.

The bass drum just bopped her softly, but it was enough. Calhoun's eyes grew wide with surprise as he saw the matronly figure of Blanche Hodel coming down on him. Her scream was muffled by the strident music of John Philip Sousa, the march king.

The bowling alley was like bowling alleys everywhere. Long polished hardwood lanes, beer signs, people dressed in identical T-shirts, a stall for renting shoes, a snack bar that sold greasy burgers, and, off in a corner, a red imitation-leather padded door to a small bar.

Nogerilli barged in first, pushing against the heavy glass door and gesturing his cohorts onward. They stomped toward the center lanes, swaggering and surly, aware of the eyes on them. A startled couple in their path quickly moved out of the way and let the gleefully villainous T-birds have the lane without argument.

"Let's bowl!" shouted Nogerilli.

Goose thumbed some money into an old jukebox and pressed the tabs. By the time he had joined the others, a "Woolly Bully" song was blasting the air, echoing off the hard surfaces.

Goose was first to grab a ball, swinging it back and up with abandon, letting out a fierce rebel yell as he threw it in the general direction of the other end of the lanes.

The big black ball struck the hardwood lane about halfway down, veered through the gutter, and thundered into the next lane for a strike. Goose stared at what he had accomplished. He looked to his right. Three sorority girls stared at him, one with a ball held back and ready to throw. Two nuns looked at him in surprise, and some older men from a hardware store bowling team blinked in disbelief.

Goose looked the other way, but a pair of rival teams from two different oil companies were also staring. An old man and his grandson were bewildered. Goose looked at Nogerilli.

"How do I score *that*?" Dimucci asked, tossing the pencil down on the score sheet.

Goose grinned. "A strike," he said proudly. "What else, jerk."

Nogerilli stared belligerently toward the entrance. "Where are the chicks?" he growled. "I said eight bells."

Davey picked up a ball and ran up to the line. He swung back the heavy black sphere, but lost his grip on it. The T-birds had only a

·fraction of a second to recognize their danger and to leap out of the path of the bowling ball. It struck the heavy bench like a cannonball, and the crash echoed throughout the lanes.

☆CHAPTER 5☆

The lights were still on at Jake's Service Station when Sharon's car wheeled into the lot, sped past the gas pumps, and came to a noisy halt by the open doors of the garage. Dolores Rebcheck looked out from the rear seat between the sweatered forms of the Pink Ladies, as Sharon called out from the driver's window.

"Would you hurry up," she yelled. "We're late and we're gonna get a warped lane, Stephanie."

They heard a muffled few words from the fluorescent depths of the concrete building. Then a hand waved from the open door of the employee's bathroom.

Dolores climbed over her sister Paulette and opened the door. "I have to go to the bathroom."

Paulette yanked her back in. "Forget it."

Sharon turned to look into the back seat. "Hey—who invited your little sister Paulette, huh?"

Dolores stuck her face out. "Who invited *you*, Sharon?"

"Here she comes," Paulette said, glad for the diversion.

Stephanie trotted out of the garage on the double. Her father came out of the office, wiping his hands on a grimy towel. He looked after her and shook his head as she jumped in. He winced as the car ground into gear and tore off.

Tom Anderson proudly indicated his trophy wall to Michael. "D Day . . . Battle of the Bulge . . . your dad and me saw 'em both, Mike."

"It must have been pretty bad," Michael nodded and looked at the trophies from the 1940s, a framed arm-patch of Patton's Third Army, and the front page of the *New York Times* on V-E Day. There were several photographs of a much younger Tom Anderson and Michael's father—grinning and slim, standing awkwardly near a burned-out Tiger tank, squatting with a grinning group of GIs, and on leave in Paris. There was a small velvet-lined box with a victory medal, a good conduct medal, and a bronze star, along with campaign ribbons; a Walther P38 automatic with a plugged barrel, which Tom Anderson had always claimed he took from a Waffen SS captain; and an enameled red-star cap device from a Russian sergeant that he outdrank—he said—in a Berlin pub.

"War is hell, son," the older man said solemnly, "but ol' Tommy Anderson wouldn't have missed that one for the world. No, sirree, Bob." He shook his head and grinned happily. "I tell you that was some war, Mike. The last great war. It had everything—good guys, bad guys, land, sea, air. They can make a million movies outta that one, I tell you, and never scratch the surface."

Michael looked at his wristwatch. "Yes, sir."

"Those English, I tell you, they were somethin'. Bombs, V-ones, V-twos, nothing stopped them. Great people, the British. Floating aircraft carrier. That was what England was, Mike. Isn't that right, mother?"

Anderson turned to his wife for confirmation. She was sitting quietly, drinking coffee. "What? What was that, dear?"

"She's heard all my stories. At least all

56

I can tell in mixed company, y'know." He winked and elbowed the boy. "I was saying England was an aircraft carrier anchored right off Hitler's front porch. Unsinkable, too, by Jim."

"Yes, dear."

Michael sneaked a look at his watch. Anderson saw him, but took his elbow anyway. "Come on, son, let me show you the fallout shelter."

"Fallout shelter, sir?"

"Uh-huh," he grinned. "Right out back. I had it put in six years ago. Stocked to the gills." He turned solemnly and put his hand on Michael's shoulder, looking him sternly in the eye. "Mike, I want your word on this. You'll not tell anyone what you are about to see."

"See, sir? What am I going to see?"

Tom Anderson pulled the student closer. "I hope to God it's never used. Let me say that right away. Never! But if it *is*," he added ominously, "I want you to know you are welcome. But just you, understand? *Just* you. You've got to promise me, boy."

"Promise you, sir?"

"That you'll not tell."

"Uh, didn't anyone see you put it in?"

"Sure, but I told them it was a cesspool. The Tripps weren't next door then. We only go out there at night, y'see. We keep it stocked, rotate the supplies, everything by the book."

"Yes, sir," Michael said, not quite understanding. "You expect a war?"

"I don't hope for one, you understand. Not like some who want to bomb the daylights out of the reds right off." He shook his head. "Nope, got to try peaceful methods first." His head came up and he stared hard at Michael. "But if they start anything, it's our duty to survive, to last, to beat 'em out."

"Sir, I—"

"Come on, Michael, it's this way. I won't turn on the back-porch light. You understand. Watch it now. Hose there, watch that. We'll go in the side door of the garage. I think I did a good job on this. Built it myself. See?" He produced a flashlight and shined it on a shelf of old boxes and some cans of oil.

"A secret door just like the movies," he said gleefully. "Shut the door behind you, Michael." The young man did it. When he turned back he saw that Mr. Anderson had swung the shelf out from the wall about two feet. "I'll just squeeze in here." He shone the light on a huge combination lock that secured a trapdoor. "I'm going to tell you the combination, Michael, but you must not tell it to a living soul, you promise?"

"Uh, yes, sir."

Anderson grinned. "It's one-seven-seven-six. Seventeen seventy-six, get it?"

"Yes, sir."

Anderson thumbed the lock and unsnapped it. "Not much room down here, son. Built it for the missus and me, but there's room for you, too. We'll make room. I used the best corrugated pipe I could get—the kind of stuff they use in highway underpasses, y'know? Concrete walls once you get in. Watch that corner now. Just squeeze in here this way."

Michael looked at his wristwatch. "Yes, sir," he sighed.

The parking lot of the bowling alley was half full when Sharon steered her car into the lot. They parked near the T-birds' machines and hopped out, tugging down skirts and adjusting straps. Dolores carried her skateboard in with her rather than leave it in the car.

They went in and sat on the benches behind the approach to put on their bowling shoes. The T-birds pointedly ignored them. Nogerilli hefted a ball, swaggered up to the foul line, eyed the cluster of white pins aggressively, then stepped back to fire the ball down the alley.

"A Woolworth!" Goose yelped, seeing the five and ten pins still standing.

"Way to go, Johnny!" Paulette said happily. She jumped up and grabbed him as he strutted back.

"Do not mess with the hair," he said, checking the spit curl carefully plastered to the center of his forehead. He put out his hand. "Comb."

Goose slapped the comb into his hand dutifully, and Johnny combed his D.A. carefully, eyeing the Pink Ladies.

"Whose side are you on, Paulette?" Sharon asked as she came down into the next alley.

"*Our* side," Paulette answered.

"Then don't fraternize with the enemy," Rhonda snapped.

"Mark that a strike," Nogerilli said, pointing at Stephanie, who had sat down in the scorekeeper's seat.

"What are you talkin' about?" she said, pointing at the end of the alley. "You missed a couple of lousy pins."

"That is a technical strike," Nogerilli said loftily, "due to the fact that you chicks was late. Read your bowlin' rules."

Stephanie looked disgusted and made an angry mark on the scorecard. Nogerilli grinned.

Rhonda picked up a ball, almost dropped it, then walked up to the foul line to examine the target of pins through slitted eyes.

"I wish she'd get glasses," Paulette muttered to her sister.

The younger girl pulled surreptitiously at her brassiere. "This bra is killing me," she whispered.

"You wish," Paulette said.

Rhonda sent her ball down the lane for a pocket split.

"Atta girl!" Paulette cried out and got up to wait for the returning ball.

Dolores leaned across the dividing bench between the Pink Ladies and the T-birds. "Got a smoke?" she asked Davey.

He frowned at her. "That'll stunt your growth, twoip."

She lifted her nose and looked him up and down haughtily. "You should know . . . twoip." She twisted around to give her attention to her sister as she stepped up to the line.

Nogerilli snorted as he saw Paulette's style. "Hey, Paulette! You gotta put your fingers in the holes!"

They all looked at the two-handed grip the leggy blonde had on the ball and laughed. "I'm not breaking my nails!" she said. "Not for no lousy bowling date, anyway!"

She moved back and forth, holding the ball, bent over, with her rear end projected and her long legs silken and smooth coming out of her shorts. Some guys in the next lane stopped to watch the swing and sway of her figure. One of them dropped his ball from his fingers and yelped as it bounced off his foot.

The T-birds had also stopped, looking at the provocative moves of the blonde. Their expressions were of lewd appreciation for the exhibition that was being put on for their benefit.

Dimucci muttered to Nogerilli, "You got something going with Paulette?"

Nogerilli let his grin change suggestively into a leer. "Let's just say I'm giving her therapy."

They watched Paulette's ball roll down the alley for a Christmas-tree hit. Paulette made an angry gesture and waited impatiently for the ball to return.

A few moments later, Dolores had her turn. To everyone's surprise she had a strike on the first time out.

"I got a strike!" she exclaimed, jumping around excitedly. "I got a strike! What's the final score?"

Nogerilli reached over and grabbed Paulette. "The *final* score happens later tonight." She nodded, bright-eyed. "Last game comin' up. Winner takes all." He grinned viciously across at the rest of the Pink Ladies. "Agreed?"

"Shoot the ball!" Rhonda cried.

"Bowl!" they all yelled enthusiastically.

☆CHAPTER 6☆

Stephanie tossed her rented shoes into Dolores's arms and made a rude, grunting sound. Davey walked by, holding out the scorecard ostentatiously, checking off what they all knew.

"Ah . . . another well-deserved victory," he said.

"So where's the trophy?" Nogerilli grinned.

"Right here, Johnny," Paulette said, pushing up against him and taking his head between her hands to give him a big kiss. He started to pull her hands down from his hair, but she pressed herself against him so firmly that he decided just to embrace her rounded body.

"Ohhh," Goose said with a wide grin.

Michael was holding the book *Bowling* to catch the streetlight as he walked along. He was muttering to himself, repeating the passages, commiting them to memory. "Always be courteous when asking for a game. Hi, want a game?" He tried another tone. "Howdy, fellas, let's bowl some balls!"

A car screeched and slid as Michael stepped out into the street, cutting across to Bowl-A-Rama, but he never noticed it.

"Bowling, anyone?" he said, putting a lot of perkiness into it. A semi-trailer made a deep-throated roar and went by, ruffling his hair. "Anyone for a few frames?"

Hooonnnnkkk!

Nogerilli finally shoved Paulette back. Everyone was staring in awe. Nogerilli gave them a cool appraisal, then looked back at the breathless and thoroughly conquered blonde. "That's for best average," he said. "Now what about best score?"

Without warning, he reached out and grabbed Stephanie's arm. "Hey!" she said, twisting in vain, then pulling her arm free.

"Touchy," Nogerilli said, raising his hand daintily. Paulette looked from Johnny to Stephanie.

Goose grinned at Stephanie. "What's the

trophy for best score of the evening?"

"I ain't no one's trophy," Stephanie snapped.

"Ooooo," Nogerilli grimaced. "She ain't no one's trophy. Miss Independent."

Stephanie glared at him. "Yeah, independent. I kiss who I want to kiss when I want to kiss."

"Oooo," the Pink Ladies said.

Stephanie's chin came up. "As a matter of fact," she said haughtily, "I could kiss . . ." She looked over the T-birds with a raised eyebrow and they licked their lips in anticipation. She had their attention, but suddenly turned and pointed at the main entrance. ". . . the next guy who walks through that door."

Everyone looked at the door.

An old man was struggling drunkenly to open the heavy oak and glass doors.

"Be my guest," leered Nogerilli, crossing his arms.

The old drunk staggered back and pulled the door outwards. From the darkness of the parking lot stepped Michael Carrington. "Thank you," he said politely to the drunk and stepped into the bowling alley.

Stephanie blinked.

Nogerilli's mouth turned down.

The beautiful blonde squared her shoulders, stepped briskly across the floor, and strutted right up to Michael, who stopped when he saw her.

There was a strange, almost wicked gleam in her eye, which surprised him. "Hi," he said.

Without a word, Stephanie reached up and pulled his curly head toward hers. Her lips parted and she kissed him hard and long and wickedly. Michael stood there, stunned, arms awkwardly out, unable to properly respond as her lithe, voluptuous body writhed against him.

Then, just as suddenly, he was released. Stephanie turned away, cool and smiling faintly. "Let's eat!" she said to her friends.

Dolores dropped her armload of rented shoes. "I vote for pizza," she said.

"You vote for bed," Paulette said. She pointed at the clock on the wall. "It's past ten and time you were home. So get goin'."

Dolores snarled. "Bed stinks." Her shoulders slumped. "Jeez, it's terrible being a kid."

"C'mon, we'll aim the brat toward home and then scare up some barfburgers," Sharon said.

"Can you order that in French?" Rhonda asked. They trooped out. Stephanie didn't look back at Michael, who was still more or less in the same position she had left him.

66

Nogerilli was also surprised by Stephanie's sudden kiss. Goose walked over to Michael and stuck his face out. "Want somethin'?"

Nogerilli glared at Michael, then snapped his fingers at his friends and pointed at the door. "Food," he commanded, and the four casually sauntered out.

Dolores had remained behind. "Life stinks," she pronounced, picking up her skateboard.

Michael nodded wearily before he remembered his manners. He stuck out his hand. "Hi. I'm Michael Carrington." She took his hand, shook it, and they started out together.

"Dolores Rebcheck," she said. "Commonly known as Paulette's little sister. Some jerks call me 'woodchuck' or 'upchuck,' but I prefer Dolores. Got it?"

He grinned down at her. "Got it. I'm Michael." He shoved open the door, and they saw the motorcycles thundering out after Sharon's car. "It looks like you and I don't make the grade, Dolores."

She nodded. "Yeah. With them it's all those weird codes and rules and pledges about cycles." She uttered a great sigh, pulled her sweater around her, and tucked her skateboard under her arm. "You gotta be a biker or a biker's old lady," She made a face and stuck her tongue out. "But without a cycle, *forget it*. Tees me off," she muttered.

They started walking across the parking lot. "We're both in the same boat," Michael said. "I sure can't afford a cycle without a job."

The girl nodded. "Yeah, but me, I'm willing to negotiate. I offered to be a Pink Lady mascot. It ain't the coolest job but it's a start. You'd think they'd listen." She made a negative gesture. "Forget it." She spit. "Tees me off."

Michael grinned. "I can see you're not too happy about it." He looked around. "Look, it's pretty late. I better walk you home."

She frowned up at him. "I don't need a babysitter. Okay?"

Solemnly, he said, "Then think of it as a date. Okay?"

She thought for a second, then tossed her skateboard onto the asphalt. "Why didn't you say so in the first place." He stepped on behind her and they started off.

Dolores laughed.

It was close to nine in the morning. Kids were bicycling, walking, and running in from all over. The buses were lumbering in and discharging their noisy cargos. Rhonda's car weaved around an Edsel and cut off a Ford. The Ford driver yelled something and Rhonda turned to yell back.

Wham!

Bumpers meshed. Mr. Stuart, the substitute teacher, almost had to climb on the roof of an Olds. The Pink Ladies popped out of the car and ran around to look at the damage. Mr. Stuart eased himself down and eyed the Pink Ladies with undisguised lasciviousness.

"You could have killed us, Rhonda," Sharon complained.

"Yeah," Paulette added. "Can you imagine dying so young?" They all rolled their eyes in disbelief. "Look, they're just hooked up a little," Paulette pointed out. "You two get on Sharon's bumper and the rest of us try to pull up the other."

Mr. Stuart controlled his eyes and tore himself away. He was breathing hard, his eyes glistening. He was a tall, blond, boyishly handsome man, who was years older than he looked from a distance. He marched resolutely inside, trying to control the movies running wild in his head.

Let them be in my sex education class, he prayed.

The air-raid siren started to whine, rising again and again to a crescendo.

"Attention! Attention!" It was Principal McGee's voice over the public address system. "This is a test. I repeat. This is a test."

No one paid any attention.

"Please *do not panic!* I repeat. *Do not panic!*"

Coach Calhoun and the student he was intently addressing ignored the broadcast alarm. "Nuclear war is just like football," the coach said with deep sincerity. "If the Russians got you in your own end, you throw the bomb."

In Principal McGee's tidy office, Blanche, wearing an air-raid helmet from World War II, was cranking an air-raid siren, all but deafening everyone within fifty feet. But Principal McGee huddled over the microphone.

"This is a simulated nuclear attack! Proceed to your nearest shelter," she instructed.

Blanche leaned forward to add a few words. "Boys on one side, girls on the other! Run!"

McGee gave her a disgusted look and continued to issue instructions. "I repeat. Do

70

not panic! Do . . . not . . . panic." She made a cutting gesture to Blanche and the siren died down. The principal slumped back in her chair. "It's a dirty job," she gasped, "but someone has to keep them calm."

☆CHAPTER 7☆

The T-birds slammed Eugene up against the wall with an economy of effort. His glasses were askew, his hands were high on the cream-colored walls, and there were rude hands all over him. His shoes were ripped off and shaken, his pockets turned out, and Goose McKenzie was rooting through his brown paper lunch bag.

"M-my m-mom won't give me l-lunch m-money, anymore," he said. "I swear. She says I'm a b-bad risk."

Goose looked up from the bag that he was inspecting. "What kind of sandwich is cucumbers and salami?"

Nogerilli threw the shoes down to the linoleum in disgust. "Jeez . . . listen, Eugene, ya little—"

"Uh-oh," Dimucci said, seeing Principal

McGee coming down the hall, looking into each classroom as she went. "Cheese it. The fuzz."

It was several moments before Eugene, eyes large and blinking, realized he was alone. His hands came down and he adjusted his clothing nervously.

If only I knew some judo, he thought. Took a course in something. Charles Atlas, maybe. Carried a rod. He frowned. Was that the right term? A rod? A heater? A piece? He shrugged and shoved his feet into his loafers. Boy, am I tired of it, he thought.

Eugene picked up his books and trudged down the hall, passing Miss McGee, who said, "Good morning, Eugene."

"Good morning, Miss McGee."

"Eugene," she said. She looked him up and down. "Eugene, I do wish you'd be the tiniest bit neater." She fixed his collar and patted his arm.

"Thank you, Miss McGee," he said in a tired voice and walked on.

Mr. Stuart walked up to the principal, who was watching the brightest boy in the class sulk along the corridor. "Good morning," he said.

"Oh. Oh, yes?"

"Good morning. The name's Stuart. With a 'u.' I'm a substitute for Mister . . ." He looked down at the paper in his hand. He looked up as Yvette Mason said good morning.

The tall principal grabbed Yvette's arm and started walking, indicating with a gesture that Stuart should accompany them. "Miss Mason, this is Mister . . ." She looked at the good-looking man. "Mister . . . ?"

"Stuart," he said.

"Mister Stuart," finished Miss McGee.

Yvette smiled at him, inspecting him prettily, though just as effectively as a drill sergeant. She preened herself with light touches of her fingers to her platinum hair. "Mister Stuart," she said.

Stuart smiled and made a gesture toward her head. "I like your hair, Miss Mason."

"Why, *thank* you, Mister Stuart," Yvette smiled, her eyes twinkling. Now *he* was a gentleman!

Miss McGee could hardly believe her ears and looked sharply from one to the other. Her expression was clearly a warning that there will be no shenanigans among the faculty.

"Miss Mason will help you out while you learn the ropes," Miss McGee said.

Yvette's fingertips made a quick inventory of the position of every strand of hair and she smilingly said, "It would be my pleasure, I'm sure."

"I'm sure you're sure," McGee said dryly.

Stuart was a little confused. He rechecked the slip of paper in his hand. "I . . . I'm a substitute for Mister . . ."

"Spears," Miss McGee said briskly. "Follow me." They marched down the hall, passing a boy holding his head back with a tissue to his nose.

"Nosebleed," he said thickly.

"Nurse, room eleven," Miss McGee said without stopping.

Stuart did a few fast steps to catch up with the principal, who was striding along, her eyes ceaselessly checking everything: fire extinguishers, trash in the hall, the alignment of class photos on the walls, the neatness of the bulletin boards, the condition of the linoleum, a suspicious stain near a pipe, a piece of red cloth protruding from a locker.

"I was told he . . . Mister, uh . . ."

"Spears."

"Spears had a mental breakdown," Stuart said, looking anxiously. Being a substitute teacher had its drawbacks. You got shoved into classes that had gone wild, constantly had to prove yourself to disbelieving and uncaring students, and sometimes you walked blindly into bizarre situations.

"I wouldn't call it a breakdown," Miss McGee said. "He just took too many pills and was convinced he had turned into one of his lab rats. We found him curled up in the cloakroom eating lettuce."

"I see," Stuart said, though he didn't. She had said it matter-of-factly, as though he had caught the flu.

Miss McGee stopped and indicated a door. "That's his room. Good luck." She stuck out her hand and Stuart automatically took it. "If you survive the week, we'll put your name on the door."

Before Stuart could respond, the principal had strode on, her head turning side to side, making notes. "What have I done to that poor guy," she whispered to herself. She shrugged. Some great swimmers were taught by being tossed into a lake. But the lake, she reminded herself, was seldom filled with piranha.

Stuart looked at the door, squared his shoulders, checked his narrow tie, and adjusted the books in his hands. He stepped forward confidently.

Let them know from the start who's boss, he thought. Take command at once. Later you can ease back, make exceptions, make friends, get more on a one-to-one basis.

He opened the door and walked cheerfully in, putting his books on the desk and giving the class his very best smile. "Good morning. My name is Mister Stuart. I'm your substitute teacher."

One boy, wearing a leather jacket, stood up. More followed. They started walking out. Notebooks were closed. The class streamed out, lighting cigarettes and chattering.

"Did you hear The Platters' new one? 'Harbor Lights'?"

"I like Brian Hyland's 'Itsy Bitsy Teeny Weeny Yellow Polka-Dot Bikini,'" a boy said with a leer.

"You would," the girl said.

"Brothers Four have a new album," a boy told a girl. "I got it. You wanna come over and hear it, huh?"

"And have to fight *your* four arms, no thanks."

The last of them left, and Mr. Stuart stared at the empty room.

"What did I say wrong?" he asked the empty space.

☆ ☆ ☆

The T-birds sauntered up to the display case just around the corner from the main hallway and hung their thumbs in their belts. A dusty collection of brass trophies on walnut bases was replaced by a brand-new display.

A big new sign on bright cardboard was

77

fastened across the back of the case: TALENT SHOW GRAND PRIZE. In front was a selection of long-playing record covers and another sign: 100 LPs—COUNT 'EM 100! They could see most of the album covers were empty by the way they sagged slightly. The school officials were dumb, but they were not stupid.

"That," Nogerilli said, stabbing at the display with his finger, "is why we're gonna win the talent show." He licked his lips. "One hundred long-playing albumins."

Davey's eyebrows went up. "But we got zero talent."

"Speak for yourself," Dimucci said.

"*That* kinda talent," Davey insisted, pointing.

"There's gotta be ten Roy Orbison albums in there," Goose said. He took out his comb and, in the reflection from the cabinet, combed his hair with a cigarette dangling expertly from his lips.

"Yeah, look . . . Johnny Preston, Elvis, Floyd Cramer, Peter, Paul and Mary, even Sinatra and the Kingston Trio." Davey grinned. "We can always trade off the square albums for somethin' good."

"*Square* albums?" Goose giggled.

"Yeah, who'd want square albums?" demanded Davey.

"Squares, you lunkhead. Jim Whatshisname and Dirk Whozits—those Preptone

78

jerks. Bruce Sanders. They're around," Davey said.

Nogerilli made up his mind. "We start rehearsin' tonight," he announced.

Davey and Dimucci saw Miss McGee heading toward them, and their instant reaction was to do an about face and take off. But Nogerilli and Goose didn't see her, and the T-bird leader was taking a deep drag as they confronted the frowning principal. His reaction was to flip it into his mouth, holding it between his lip and his teeth. His eyes got big.

"Mister Nogerilli, I've been looking for you," Miss McGee said sternly.

"Hello, Miss McGee," Goose said with a fake smile.

"Don't suck up, McKenzie," McGee snapped at him. Her hard look returned to the uncomfortable-looking Nogerilli. "I have received a report, Mister Nogerilli, that you have been driving your motorcycle across the school lawn."

All Nogerilli could manage was a "Mmmmmm."

"Is this true, Mister Nogerilli?" she demanded.

He shrugged and said, "Mmmmm."

She looked sternly from T-bird to T-bird. "Well, this is my first and *last* warning. No more. Am I understood?"

Nogerilli nodded. ''Mmmm . . . mmmm-mm.''

As she walked off, she sniffed the air. "Do I smell something burning?"

Goose turned at once to his leader. "You told her, Johnny," he said proudly. "Hey . . . Johnny, youse lookin' a bit sick, man . . . ."

Nogerilli's face contorted and he spat out the cigarette. He gasped hoarsely, "Water!" He ran off around the corner toward the water fountain. Goose looked at the soggy cigarette with a wisp of smoke coming up from it and shuddered.

The sign, handmade in the art department, sat on an easel in the lobby of the auditorium: TALENT SHOW TRYOUTS. WIN BIG PRIZES!! Dolores thought that two exclamation marks were tacky. You should either use one, correctly, or go whole hog and slather them across the paper to show your excitement. Two was bland.

She stepped through the rear doors of the auditorium and let her eyes adjust to the darkness. Only the stage and the first row or two had any real light. She moved along the left wall and paused near the statue of Lincoln set in a niche to watch what was happening on stage.

80

There were three sorority girls on the stage, standing ready at the edge of the dark green curtains. In the rear was the battered old rehearsal piano and, to her surprise, the English exchange student, Carrington, was sitting on the bench before it.

"Michael!" one of the sorority girls said in that too-sweet voice that sorority girls use so often. "We're ready!"

Michael turned to the keyboard, and the three girls turned on their best smiles.

She saw Miss McGee and Miss Mason sitting upright and smiling in the seats nearby with Blanche behind them. There were empty seats all around them, and Dolores slipped into one to listen.

Miss Mason said proudly, "These are *my* girls. There's very good breeding up there."

"And that's so important," Blanche breathed. McGee turned stiffly to give her assistant a stare.

Under her breath, Yvette Mason was counting the rhythm. "One and two and . . ."

Dolores couldn't take any more. She walked down the row and turned down the aisle and moved through the waiting students to the backstage. Michael and his piano were near the back curtain, almost out of sight of the audience. She slipped in next to him.

"What's happening?"

"Hey, Woodchuck," he said, his fingers plunking away, his gaze returning to the singers.

"*Dolores*, all right? What's happening?"

Michael indicated the singers with a movement of his shoulder.

Dolores looked at Michael and they both made upchucking movements.

Behind the last curtain, Sharon, Rhonda, and Stephanie were reading and re-reading their sheet music. Sharon paced frantically back and forth. "There are one hundred LPs at stake here," Sharon said earnestly to Rhonda. "And I will not let a little hard work stand between me and that prize."

She stopped and lifted her bosom proudly. "We're calendar girls. You have to get into your season. Rhonda, you're fall. Give me maturity. Give me *aging*."

Rhonda rolled her eyes and appealed to Stephanie. "Give me a break."

Stephanie nodded to Rhonda. "Lunch time," she said, twirling her finger at her temple.

The Pink Ladies could hear the sorority girls continuing in the epic saga of unrequited love involving Brad.

But Principal McGee had had enough. Wearing a smile, she sang out, "Thank you!" She waved at them, still smiling. "We haven't got all day!"

"But these are *my* girls," Yvette Mason said in surprise. She had trained and advised them. The leader was wearing *her* pearls.

"I know, dear," said Miss McGee. "Next!" she said loudly.

Sharon stuck her head through the curtain and called out into the dimness to Miss McGee, "We're almost ready!" She yanked her head back and nervously raised her hands to give the girls one more vocal run-through.

"Oo, oo, oo . . ."

"Ooo, ooo, ooo . . ."

"Let's go," she said gloomily. It hadn't been like this in all those Mickey Rooney movies about Carvel High, she thought. But then, they'd had Judy Garland or someone *good*.

The first of the calendar girls went on stage, with the rest—the months and the seasons—waiting in line. Michael got up from the piano bench and walked over to Stephanie. "Hello," he said.

She glanced at him. "Hi."

"I . . . I wanted to ask you . . ." He hesitated, noticing that all the other girls were listening. Some were grinning. "Ah, if you're . . . well . . . free after school today."

Stephanie looked up at him again. "Yeah, I'm free every day. It's in the Constitution."

Michael didn't know what to say, and the other girls were so obviously listening. He shrugged and melted away into the stacked scenery, trying to be unobtrusive. He tried to hear the song being sung on stage, but his mind kept wandering.

Michael saw Rhonda parade out with two other girls, each representing an autumn month. "If you fall in the fall you'll see September can be heavenly."

Nearby, Sharon yelled *sotto voce* to the flies high overhead. "Eugene!" Michael looked up to see the bespectacled youth perched rather precariously on the catwalk, with baskets of leaves on one side and baskets of fake snow on the other. "Ready with the leaves when I yell!"

He made a thumb and forefinger gesture, almost lost his balance, caught himself, and squeaked, "Ready!"

The eternal pageant of fall continued on stage.

The girls postured and turned, singing rather nervously, promising themselves that they'd be better when the chips were down. It seemed like an eternity out there when suddenly, Miss McGee shouted, "Thank you! That's all for today!" she added.

Sharon rushed to the edge of the side curtain. "No, wait! We have three more seasons to go!"

Miss Mason stood up as Miss McGee sidled out of the seats and went back to her office. "I'm sorry, dear, you'll have to clear the stage for the drama class."

Sharon was befuddled. All her plans were going down the drain. "No, wait, please wait! I forgot the *leaves*!"

All that Eugene heard above the noise was one word. "Coming down!" he said, tipping the big basket.

Sharon looked up, her eyes popping wide open. *"No!"*

The leaves came down in a lump, missing Sharon by inches and scattering in every direction. Sharon gave a shout of total disgust and threw her papers in the air, striding off the stage, kicking clumps of leaves before her.

"That was wonderful, girls," Blanche said, applauding.

☆CHAPTER 8☆

The Pink Ladies were packing up their things and getting ready to leave backstage. Michael detached himself from the scenery flats and walked slowly over to Stephanie. "How about a hamburger later?" he asked Stephanie.

"I'm busy," she said immediately.

Taken aback by the quick response, Michael hesitated, then tried again. "How about tomorrow?" he asked politely.

"Busy," she said.

He took a deep breath, getting slightly angry. "Then, maybe you can explain to me what happened at the bowling lanes. You just don't kiss—"

"The kiss was a joke," Stephanie said with a sharp look. "Forget it." She snatched up her books and started toward the exit, but after a few steps the hastily piled books slid apart and three of them thumped to the floor.

Coming out of his surprise, Michael stepped quickly over to her. "Let me give you a hand," he said.

"I can manage," Stephanie said. But she noticed Rhonda whispering to Paulette and pointing at her and the English student. She grabbed the books that Michael held out and hugged them to her chest. Loud enough for the other Pink Ladies to hear she said, "Hey, look, I said I could manage."

She just grabbed another book from Michael's hand, stacked it, and stood up quickly. She saw Rhonda nudge Paulette and hear her stage-whisper, "I think he's in love."

"*I* think he's sorta cute," Paulette said with a grin.

Stephanie was trying to reorganize the stack of books in her arms, but she growled at her friends, "I think you two can shut your yaps."

Paulette and Rhonda grinned, but turned to leave. Michael found one last book, a paperback dictionary, and stepped over to hold it out.

"You forgot this one." She took it and

kept on juggling the books in her arms. "How about the day after tomorrow?" he asked.

The beautiful young blonde glared at him. "Look, when are ya gonna get the picture?" Taken aback by her sudden heat, Michael just stood there. "If you really want to know what I want in a guy," she said. "Well, I'm lookin' for a dream on a mean machine . . . with *hell* in his eyes."

She stopped and turned away abruptly. "Cool rider," she almost whispered. "If he's cool enough he can burn me through and through." She seemed to be talking to herself, and it embarrassed Michael.

"If it takes forever, then I'll wait forever. No ordinary boy is gonna do," she said, giving him a swift up-and-down look.

Dimucci stepped out from behind a curtain and sauntered over to put his arm around Michael's shoulder in a suspiciously friendly manner, but the English youth hardly noticed. He watched Stephanie as she turned and walked right past him and Dimucci, ignoring them, to pick up her books.

Michael watched her go by, and a few seconds passed before he realized Dimucci had been talking to him for some time. "What I'm sayin' is, you're Mister History around here and like I got this essay on the fall of Rome, y'know?" He shrugged and grinned. "I didn't even know they were in trouble."

Michael forced his attention to the dark-haired T-bird. "What are you driving at, Dimucci?"

The leather-jacketed youth grinned and rubbed his hands together in the universal symbol for money. "Papers for paper, essays for cash."

Stephanie had managed her armload of books into a proper stack and strode by them again without batting an eye or acknowledging their existence.

Almost to himself Michael said, "So that's it."

"What's it?" Dimucci asked.

"It's got to be a motorcycle," Michael muttered.

Dimucci had still not caught on, but he nodded. "Good idea. Invest the loot in a cycle. So?"

Carrington turned to the T-bird and nodded. "You've got a deal."

"All *right*!" Dimucci said. Then his grin faded and he looked around suspiciously. "But listen, we gotta be cool. When we make the drop, we can't do it in the open like this, okay? I got a rep to protect."

Michael nodded absently.

Michael was working in Tom Anderson's fallout shelter where the late-night pounding of the typewriter wouldn't bother anyone. He had restacked some crates of canned goods and put a couple of heavy boards across to make a desk. The surface was littered with notes, paper, books with strips of paper marking passages, and some pens.

He typed out a final quote—Gibbon, of course—and added the final sheet to the stack to the right of the typewriter. He turned the stack over and read the title page, "Why Rome Fell, by Louis Dimucci," and smiled wryly.

Michael looked up as he heard steps on the ladder coming down from the garage. "Hullo," Dimucci said, ducking into the shelter. He looked around with surprise. "What is this joint?"

"A nuclear fallout shelter."

"That you?" Dimucci said, shading his eyes from the light from the gooseneck lamp.

"You got the money?" Michael asked.

"Yeah," Dimucci said, digging into his pocket as he looked around. "This is a neat joint. Secret entrance like a Saturday serial 'n' everything."

He began to dump crumpled bills onto the improvised desk top, adding a lot of loose change.

Michael said, "Keep quiet about this place, okay?"

"Sure, sure," Dimucci said. "Everyone's got secrets."

Michael handed him the sheaf of paper. "Here it is."

"Jeez," Dimucci said, looking at it. "You misspell those words I gave you? I always misspell those words. I dunno why. Don't want anyone to get suspicious."

"I did it right," Michael said, gathering up the crumpled bills and smoothing them out as he counted.

☆ ☆ ☆

In the boys washroom, Michael Carrington and Goose McKenzie were crowded into one of the cubicles. Goose took an essay from Michael and handed him some folded bills. "Can you handle a couple of history assignments, too?"

Michael shrugged. "I'll try."

Goose frowned hard at him. "Remember, this is between us, okay? I gotta rep to protect, y'know."

Michael nodded. All of his inventory of "clients" had reputations.

At that moment, the cubicle door was swung open and Eugene started in, unbuckling his pants. He saw the two of them and his jaw dropped. He turned white. The calculus book under his arm flopped to the tiles as he turned around and trotted off in a hurry.

"Holy Moses," he muttered. "My mother was right."

Every evening, in the fallout shelter, Michael hunched over the typewriter. He had bought a whole ream of paper at the school supply store and it was being noticeably reduced. There was a selection of books nearby on a crate of canned beans and he had found a better chair—one with a cushion.

This one's the front wheel, he thought. Then that short essay for Davey Jaworski would get him the seat.

His fingers thumped away on the keys.

Nogerilli sauntered insolently into the corridor made by the high chain link fencing and leaned coolly against the wire. A cigarette dangled from his lips. He fingered the money in his jacket pocket and waited impatiently.

He saw Michael Carrington coming along by the gym, then turn into the passage. There was a notebook under his arm. As he approached, Michael pulled out a thin sheaf of typed sheets fastened with a paper clip. Nogerilli took it and stuffed it unceremoniously into his unzipped jacket. In the same motion, he slapped the cash into Michael's hand.

"Nobody, but *nobody* knows this happened, right?" he asked.

"Whatever you say," Michael shrugged.

Nogerilli grunted and started off in the other direction. "Right. 'Cause I got a rep to protect. Dig?"

"Dig," Michael said to himself and smiled.

The shop was small, grubby and cluttered. Even the sign, Pfeil's Cycle Shop, was grimy. The bearded owner was covered in grease, but his eyes glittered as he saw the pile of money being dumped on the counter. The bills were crumpled and there was a lot of silver, but they quickly stacked the money

93

in piles and it came out to the right sum.

"That's my down payment," Michael Carrington said.

The owner swept the folding money into a wad and made it disappear into his pocket. He indicated a pile of motorcycle parts lying nearby. "You got yourself a bike, fella."

☆ ☆ ☆

The Pink Ladies exited Mr. Stuart's classroom, giggling, with the T-birds sauntering along behind, grinning. "I don't believe it," Sharon said. "Mister Stuart got all hot and bothered when he started explaining reproduction."

"Gross," Paulette announced.

"*Gross*," Rhonda agreed.

"He's cute, though, kinda," Sharon added. "I mean, for an older man."

"And Miss Mason auditing the class," Stephanie said. "That was somethin' interestin', huh?"

"When you get that old," Rhonda wondered, "do you still want to . . . uh . . . you know?"

"How do I know?" Stephanie said. "I'm never getting *that* old."

"Ho-ho," Sharon and Rhonda said.

"Consider the alternative," Paulette grinned.

Davey Jaworski pulled away from the leather ranks of the T-birds and pulled Michael Carrington aside, nervously tugging at his sleeve. "Hey, come here."

"What do *you* want?"

Davey looked around carefully. "Look, uh, I gotta do this dumb essay on hygiene. This is strictly between you and me, see, 'cause—"

"You've got a rep to protect," Michael finished dryly.

Davey was a bit surprised by Michael's astuteness. "Yeah, uh, right." He grinned and reached up to put an arm around Michael's shoulder as they walked down the echoing corridor.

☆CHAPTER 9☆

Michael stepped back and looked the motorcycle over. He wore greasy overalls and his hair was rumpled, but there was a wide smile of satisfaction on his face as he inspected the machine.

It was made up of spare parts, salvaged parts, and a few new parts. Starting with a good frame from a wrecked Harley, Michael had put the whole thing together himself.

He thought everything was right, but there was only one way to find out. He swung a long leg over the machine and sat down. He turned the key and stood up to kick down hard on the starter.

The young Englishman revved it up, then twisted the grip to put it in gear. The engine roared and it took off. The cycle moved two yards and locked.

It's September 1960 and the beginning
of another terrifying year at Rydell for
Blanche and Principal McGee

The T-Birds rev up for Senior Year

Frenchy, the beauty-school dropout,
introduces handsome Londoner Michael
Carrington to Rydell

Nogerelli and Paulette find their
happy ending

Stephanie and Michael graduate...
and start a new life together

Michael went over the handlebars and slammed up against the back wall of Pfeil's Cycle Shop. He heard the engine stall out and stop. Then a woman's hand extended into his range of vision and he looked up to see Frenchy Lefevre.

"What are you trying to do, Michael?"

He smiled wryly. "I'm trying to ride this bike without bloody well killing myself."

He got up without her help, dusted his hands, and grunted as he heaved the big machine upright. He kick-started it again, revved it up, and sat down.

"Wait a second, Michael, this isn't for—" But he released the clutch and took off as Frenchy finished her sentence: "Stephanie. . . ."

Ka-boom!

Frenchy winced.

☆ ☆ ☆

There were a couple of Band-Aids on Michael's fingers as they raced over the typewriter keys. The title page was, "Sex, Morality, and the Animal Kingdom, by David F. Jaworski."

He took the sheet out and laid it down, then picked up the next sheet and inserted it into the typewriter. He was going to need a new ribbon soon.

"Sex," he typed.

Coach Calhoun came into the principal's outer office at a trot, sweat-stained and rumpled, and began going through his teacher's mailbox. The school copy of *Sports Illustrated* was there, the one he was supposed to pass on to the library and rarely did. A letter from Voit, a catalog from another sporting-goods company, a postcard from a kid he had said would never play good ball who was now second string with the Baltimore Orioles.

He turned and saw Blanche behind an open filing cabinet, waving at him. "Good morning, Blanche. All quiet on the western front?" He then realized she was waving him over. "That big?" he said as he went over to the filing cabinet.

She leaned across to whisper. "Something *awful* must have happened in sex ed." She looked around at the principal's door. "Miss McGee is simply beside herself."

"A strange position," Calhoun frowned.

"No, she's really upset."

"Sex is just like football, Blanche. If you're in trouble, punt."

"I don't know why we need to teach sex in the schools, anyway," Blanche complained. "I never had sex in school and look at me." With a certain amount of anger she slammed shut the filing cabinet—on Calhoun's fingers.

"Blanche," Calhoun winced. But she hadn't seen what she had done.

She blinked at him seductively and smiled, "Yes?"

"Blanche," he said in a strangled voice, "you don't know what you're doing to me."

"Oh, Mister Cal*houn* . . ."

"Blanche . . ."

"Yes," she simpered.

"My hand!" the coach exploded.

She blinked in consternation as she saw his predicament, her hands fluttering. "Oh, you should be more careful," she said, releasing his hand.

Calhoun exited, holding his wounded hand. "Blanche," he sighed. "You're a health hazard."

Miss McGee opened her office door and let Mr. Stuart precede her into the outer office. He looked nervous and chastened.

"Just remember, Mister Stuart, that

99

their bodies are more developed than their minds."

"I understand," Stuart said, well aware of the development of at least one of the students.

"They have drives, Mister Stuart."

"I understand," he said, knowing they were not the only ones.

"*Lustful* drives, Mister Stuart."

"I understand," Stuart repeated.

"Good," Miss McGee said briskly, stepping over to pick up a supply inventory from Blanche's desk.

☆ ☆ ☆

Michael was at the rehearsal piano, and the Preptones were on stage, singing "Mr. Sandman." Nogerilli appeared out of the backstage shadows and came up to the piano. Michael looked pointedly at his notebook lying on top. Nogerilli's hand went in, left cash, and slipped out the clipped sheaf of papers, stuffing them into his shirt. He swaggered away without looking back.

Yvette Mason smiled happily from the seats, the odor of hair spray filling the air around her. "Those are my boys," she said to the principal seated next to her. "Clean, upright, American boys."

"I know, dear," Miss McGee said. Her voice cut through the singing. "Thank you, next! The T-bones!"

Nogerilli bellowed impatiently from backstage. "That's *T-birds!*"

Miss McGee smiled at Miss Mason. "These are *my boys*."

The T-birds came straggling on, self-consciously overdoing their usual cool act.

"Well, come on and tell us, Johnny," Goose sang huskily.

"What's the secret of success?" Dimucci smirked.

Nogerilli hitched up his belt.

Miss McGee's smile began to fade, then set rather primly as the T-bird's song progressed. It was all about the place where guys—guys who were super-cool like T-birds—were guaranteed to score.

It turned out to be the grocery store.

There was something about a female butcher.

And walking like a T-bird, which to Miss McGee's mind meant swaggering, stiff-legged macho parades.

"Thank you!" she managed to sing out at last, putting all her twenty-seven years of teaching ability into making it sound appreciative.

"That was *won*-der-ful!" Blanche called out, clapping furiously. But backstage Nogerilli was slapping the other T-birds around for messing up.

"Calendar girls!" Miss McGee called out.

After a few moments of confusion, Stephanie came on stage in her "winter" costume, along with the back-up singers, which included Paulette, making the most of her costume's skimpiness.

The song was about being a girl for all seasons, and they paraded around as they sang. Paulette gave it everything she had, and was very sexy, especially when she saw Johnny Nogerilli standing in the wings.

He whispered at her intently, "Paulette, we *know* you're blessed with the goods, but you don't have to bless the whole school. *That,*" he frowned, "is for my eyes only, got it?"

Paulette's response was just to look lovingly at Johnny and glide on by, still moving her lithe body to the music. The T-bird leader groaned and glowered.

Sharon, who had been monitoring the performance from the wings, hissed at Paulette. "No talking in back."

"Thank you," Miss McGee said.

Sharon clenched her fists. "No!" she exclaimed. "We've still got two seasons!"

"That's all for today," Miss Mason called out.

Sharon threw her script in the air in frustration. "It's like being bit to death by a *duck!*" she growled and stomped off.

"Ouch!" Sharon gasped, hitting her shin on some obstruction in the dark.

Lou Dimucci hissed back, insisting on her silence. The backyard of the Anderson home was quite dark, with just a little light coming from an upstairs window and a neighbor's shaded bedroom window. They could hear a small dog yapping somewhere.

"I don't know how you talked me into this, Louis," Sharon Cooper whispered.

"Yeah, yeah," Dimucci whispered back, feeling his way along. "Listen, you trust President Kennedy, right?"

"Of course," she said, patting her dark hair where a pillbox hat should have been. However, she didn't think Jacqueline Bouvier Kennedy would be sneaking into a garage in the middle of the night.

"C'mon," whispered Dimucci, pulling her into the open garage. He tiptoed along the wall to the shelf and pulled it out, stopping when he heard the squeak. They waited, but there was no alarm, so he pulled out a screwdriver and went to work on the padlock.

After a moment's work, Sharon heard the lock rip loose. Then Lou whispered as he took her elbow, "Well, listen, Kennedy says we gotta be prepared for a nucleoid war, right?"

"Nuclear, Louis."

"Whatever. Get in here." He guided her into the passage, glancing back to see a dark figure trot silently up the driveway and melt into the bushes. He smiled and followed Sharon down the ladder.

Goose followed Davey up the driveway and set down the portable air-raid siren. They waited a few seconds, then sneaked into the garage and set the siren down next to the hidden entrance.

A match flared in the dark as they sat back to give Dimucci a few moments to get ready. They lit cigarettes and waited.

Dimucci snapped the lights on and happily jumped on the lower bunk bed, bouncing up and down. Sharon looked around, taking in the stacks of canned goods, cartons of toilet paper, kerosene lamp, typewriter, and medical kit.

"This is an official fallout shelter bed," Dimucci said.

Sharon sat down next to him and bounced on it, her manner experimental and cautious.

"Like you gotta be prepared," he said. "Because some day, when you least expect it—*ka-blam!* Nucleoid war!"

Sharon nodded and looked around. Images appeared in her head of immense mushroom clouds, GIs in gas masks, and people running for shelters. She shivered, then sat up straight, eyes bulging, as an air-raid siren shrilled through the night.

The frightened girl grabbed Dimucci, who could barely keep a straight face. "What's that?"

"It's started!" he said, trying to scare her. He stiffened on the bed. "Our country's calling. The *unimaginabobble* has happened."

"What's started?" Sharon gasped. "What's *happening?*"

"The Russians are attacking!" Dimucci exclaimed, pulling her down on the bed. "Get down!" He looked fearfully at the concrete ceiling. "Hear that?" he said over the sound of the wailing siren.

"Hear *what*?"

"The bombs. Far off, but—" He broke off to listen hard.

"Louis, I—"

"Hear that? Hear that?"

"You crazy?" Dimucci exclaimed, glancing up toward the noise. "They're droppin' *bombs* out there!" Sharon silently continued her fight to get out from under.

"Listen," Lou said hotly, "we gotta do it for the red, the white, and the blue, babe. It's ol' Uncle *Sam* who's doin' the askin'." He patted her shoulder. "Don't worry, our folks will understand, they'll approve, considerin' the circumstances."

Sharon's struggles lessened somewhat. "Tomorrow, I'll . . ." Lou put a choke in his voice. "I'll be in the fightin'. But I'll win this crazy war . . . for you." He pressed tighter against her. "There's priorities in wartime, Sharon. People make sacrifices. Our country . . . well, our good ol' U.S. of A. wants us to."

"Oh, Lou, I—"

Bullets are flyin'," he said with becoming modesty. "Bombs goin' bang. They'll be here soon. Things move fast in modern war. Give that somethin' to the United States of America that you never gave before," he said earnestly.

Sharon's face brightened. "You sure my

mother would, you know, approve?"

"Your mother doesn't havta know, Sharon," Lou said knowingly.

"And . . . and you think we're old enough to go?"

Dimucci looked around furtively, hiding a grin. "All the way," he said huskily. "Think of it, Sharon, baby. We'll be doin' it for the Constitution, the right of free speech . . ."

"The Grand Canyon," she sighed, pressing against him.

"The Dodgers! The Yankees!" he shouted.

"Disneyland!" she gasped. He hugged her more.

"For our country, this great land of ours, the land that gave us Thomas Jefferson and Elvis Presley!" Sharon said in a shaky voice.

"We *owe* it to our country," Lou breathed.

"Then . . . then . . . let's *do* it for our country," she said with breathless determination.

"Uncle Sam wants us to," Lou added smugly.

They paused. This was an important moment. They looked deep into each other's eyes. "I'm ready, Louis," she said.

To his surprise, she had put on an army helmet and was standing virtually at attention. "Then let's sign up!" she said, the light of patriotism blazed from her face.

"No, wait!" he said as she turned toward the ladder. "Hey, Sharon, no, wait—!"

She scrambled up the ladder and opened the trapdoor.

And Goose and Davey both fell in.

☆CHAPTER 10☆

The cycle was newly painted and polished. The almost-new tires had been painted, too, and the leather seat rubbed with oil. It was a beauty.

Michael couldn't help it. He jumped on it quickly, fired it up, and took off.

He did a wheelie along the street and dropped to the ground just in time to make a turn into a big vacant lot. He swung the bike up, raising a cloud of dust as he did another tricky wheelie.

Suddenly, there was someone in front of him. Michael swerved and dropped the front wheel down as the figure dove through the dust to avoid him. Michael turned around and killed the engine. The dust drifted off and he saw Frenchy Lefevre getting to her feet.

"You all right?" Michael asked.

"I can't believe that was you," she said, waving a hand before her face and blowing.

He grinned. "I've been practicing. You *sure* you're okay?"

"Yeah, yeah," she said, fumbling with a wrapped package. "I got something for you." She ripped the paper and extracted a pair of black leather trousers and held them out to him.

"What's that?" he asked, a bit confused.

"What's it look like? Leather pants. I whipped 'em up in the sewing room."

"For *me*?"

"No, for Eugene," she said dryly. She waggled the garment at him. "Of course, for you. As long as you got this ridiculous idea in your head, I figure you better go in guns blazing. If you know what I mean."

Michael took them, holding them at arm's length. "Me . . . in those?" he said.

"They'll fit," she said. "I borrowed a pair of your well-worn denims from Mrs. Anderson. The leather was left over from a project from last year."

"Me . . . in these . . .?" Michael said.

Dolores gave the sidewalk another push with her left foot, and angled her skateboard into the parking lot of Bowl-A-Rama lanes. She immediately spotted Balmudo astride his motorcycle, engine running, but with none of the other Cycle Lords in sight.

Dolores raised her chin and looked as regal and as cool as possible as she sailed right by, deftly avoiding a beer bottle. Her forearm was raised in the classiest of defiant gestures.

"Creep," she said under her breath.

She hopped off at the alley door, scooped up her skateboard, and pushed inside without looking back.

Balmudo raised his arm and snapped his fingers.

Dolores trotted into the echoing bowling alley and looked quickly around. She spotted her sister Paulette getting some drinks at the counter and the rest of the Pink Ladies in a booth just behind the pinball machine where three of the T-birds were assembled.

She ran over to them and announced breathlessly, "Balmudo's out front and he's all alone!"

Nogerilli heard her but his expression didn't change. He leaned hard into the pinball machine and pounded on the side. The machine lit up: *TILT!*

"Tilt," Goose said. "My turn."

Nogerilli turned away lazily. "Your turn after we tilt that craterface, Balmudo." He

111

started for the door. "Come on with me."

Goose abandoned the pinball machine and joined Dimucci as they all strutted out of the restaurant area, playing it very tough, pushing through the crowd. The Pink Ladies slid out of the booth and followed. "You stay here," Paulette said to her sister, who didn't listen to her.

Nogerilli stopped just before the exit, holding out a hand. "Comb," he said.

Nogerilli combed his hair carefully, giving the spitcurl one last twist. He handed back the comb and said, "Smoke."

Goose was ready for him. "Light," Nogerilli said, waiting. Dimucci flipped his Zippo and ignited the end of Johnny's drooping cigarette. The T-bird leader insolently blew out a cloud of smoke and resumed his advance.

The three T-birds burst through the doors into the parking lot and stopped. Fifteen Cycle Lords sat astride their bikes in a semi-circle around the door, with Balmudo in the middle, grinning viciously.

"Comb again," Nogerilli said.

They all pulled out combs and stepped quickly back through the still-moving door.

Dolores had started to run for the side exit, knowing that Paulette would ground her if she saw her go out the front. But she ran into Davey Jaworski coming out of the men's room. She grabbed his arm.

"Come on! Action out front!" she exclaimed.

"What?"

"Balmudo is going to get his face mangled!"

They started back toward the front doors, pushing through the group of bowlers trying to get a look. Because they were short, neither Davey nor Dolores saw the rest of the T-birds back inside on the other side of the wide entrance.

Davey shoved through the door belligerently, yelling out, "Where's that ratface, Balmuuu . . ."

His voice died and he gulped. He stared at the semi-circle of bikers. They were all off their bikes and advancing toward the bowling alley. Balmudo reached out and grabbed Davey's jacket, throwing him hard against the door frame.

The other Cycle Lords marched in slowly, savoring the moment. A chain jingled in a gloved hand. A switchblade clicked open. A gloved fist smacked into a gloved palm.

Then there came the roar of a powerful engine from the alley, and a Cycle Lord snapped his head around. He saw only a blur as a headlight flashed on, reflecting off the cyclist's goggles. The machine thundered in, striking between Davey and Balmudo, making them both shrink back.

"What the *hell!*" a Lord exclaimed.

The mystery biker whipped his machine sideways and stopped. He looked back and seemed to dare the Lords to chase him.

"Who the hell is *that?*" one of the gang growled, rolling a chain around his fist.

"Get that guy!" Balmudo ordered.

The Lords scrambled to get aboard their bikes and rev them up. The mystery biker rolled slowly and insolently out of the lot and gunned it in the street as the deep-throated roar of the pack sounded.

"Who the hell was *that?*" Davey muttered.

Michael Carrington grinned under his helmet, then twisted the grip, bringing the engine noise to a screaming pitch.

The Cycle Lords shot out of the lot like watermelon seeds spit into the night. They yelled as they burned rubber in pursuit.

The T-birds came out and joined Davey in the lot, shaken from the near-disaster of four against fifteen.

"He just shot outta nowhere," Davey said, pointing. "Just blazin' by like a rocket pilot!"

"That's some kinda natural-born bike jockey," Goose said. "He burned up the pavement with those wheels o' his."

The Cycle Lords all took a corner sharply, slanted over and firing high. "He's lookin' for a rumble," one of the Lords shouted. "And he came to the right party!"

"He's gonna do a header," another yelled, raising his fist to the sky, "with one punch o' this steel."

"The only thing you guys are gonna do," shouted the Pink Ladies in the parking lot, "is eat his *dust!*"

"Who's that guy?" they all asked each other and shrugged.

"Where did he *come* from?" Paulette asked.

"Who can that crazy dude be?" Sharon muttered.

"Hey," Nogerilli growled, "who's this new kid on the block, huh? Spill it—any o' you guys know?"

"Nope," Goose said, giving Sharon a dark look. Then he squinted in the direction of the fading sounds. "I wonder who . . ."

A Cycle Lord yelled across to his buddy as they streaked through an intersection, following the mystery cyclist's taillights. "That joker's got some hot machine," he admitted reluctantly, "but it ain't hot enough for the Lords!"

The Cycle Lords raced across a vacant

lot into an alley and thumped out into the street, causing a car to screech to a stop.

"We're gonna wrap those handlebars around that neck o' his!" Balmudo vowed loudly. "The punk will get it!"

☆CHAPTER 11☆

Nogerilli glared sullenly about him with jealousy eating at his heart. They never did anything like this for me, he thought, looking at the excitement, hearing the distant thunder of the cycles.

Goose and Dimucci let their excitement cool off, seeing Johnny Nogerilli's bitter calm. But Davey Jaworski was pretty excited. After all, the mysterious biker had saved him from a terrible fate—getting beaten up by the Cycle Lords.

Rhonda shivered. "That guy could *move!*"

"Okay, no kidding around," Davey said, "Who *is* he?"

"You don't get that good overnight," Stephanie sighed.

Davey stepped out, swaggering. "Couldn't see his face . . ."

Stephanie joined him, hip to hip. "It really doesn't matter that I haven't seen his face."

"When we find out who he is . . ." Goose muttered. In truth, he was a bit confused. The rider had saved Davey from a prime bashing, but, on the other hand, it was an intrusion on the T-birds' turf. Cycle Lords and T-birds understood each other, but this was a wild card, a third party. Was there a new gang around or just a foolish loner out to make a name by taking on the top guns?

Careening around a truck, Michael led the Lords in a frantic chase of spinning wheels and flashing lights. He remembered the cheers and cries as he had raced out of the parking lot. They want me, he thought. Everybody wants you when they don't know who you are, he thought bitterly.

Michael went into a driveway, along the sidewalk, past garbage cans, and back into the street to flash up a dark alley, with the gang behind him. Lights were turned on in windows as the night thunder rolled past.

"Take a look around you," Michael muttered to himself, downshifting and turning down the next street. He heard the Cycle Lords come into the alley. "Michael, me boy . . . you're a star. Everyone wants you . . . but for different reasons."

The charging beasts of steel and rubber, gasoline-breathing dragons with their rusty knights astride, thundered through the night.

Michael's motorcycle almost went into a skid as he rammed the machine sideways for a sudden turn into another street. He straightened out, wondering just how he had gotten himself into this and how he was going to get out.

His act had been impulsive. He didn't think beyond saving the smallest T-bird and pulling the other gang off into the night, away from the outnumbered T-birds. He crouched as low as he could, "getting under the paint" as the bikers called it, and raced down the street.

They never knew that I could be so cool, he thought. A little smile came to his lips. But then a station wagon pulled out from a sidestreet and Michael had to think fast to get around it.

And behind him, jouncing and yelling, came the Cycle Lords, erupting from an alley.

I bet they think it's Brando, Michael thought. They don't know it's just the limey,

Michael. He was a bit in awe of himself at that moment by doing something he had not thought he was capable of. But the motorcycle seemed like a part of him, a natural extension of his body. And saving Davey seemed natural, too. Inevitable, he thought. Fate. Kismet. I had to. I couldn't *not* do it.

"Know what?" he asked himself with a grin, "even if they catch you—you've won."

Michael was aware of a distant police siren but it didn't bother him. He was on wings—sailing on the night thunder—invulnerable and free.

The alley that he turned into was a dead end. He screeched as he slowed, then whipped the bike around, spitting water and trash from under the wheels, and raced back down the alley.

The Cycle Lords were closer, their screams changing from rage to triumph. "Get that clown!" Balmudo cried as Michael whipped the bike around and gunned it up the street.

A trio of Cycle Lords was cutting in from another street, sliding sideways to form a wall of metal across his path. Michael braked, rammed over a curb, almost clipped a mail box, and thumped back out into the street just past the blockers.

Tires squealed, motors roared, leathered arms waved, and curses filled the night.

Michael made a left at Elm and headed back for Bowl-A-Rama with the mob in pursuit.

"What now?" he asked aloud.

He could see the tall neon flash of the bowling alley a few blocks ahead and headed for it, an island of light in a sea of darkness. He braked and turned into the lot, but he hadn't lost the pursuers. Their clamoring engines came down the street as he whipped the bike around and aimed for another exit.

But they cut him off. He went toward the back of the building, where the loading ramps and empty stacked crates were. He had only the shortest moment to notice the black leather T-birds at the entrance and the brighter colors of the Pink Ladies, plus a few gawking spectators behind them.

A police car came around the corner and wailed into the parking lot just behind the Cycle Lords.

Michael found the alleyway blocked by a tractorless produce trailer parked across the exit next to the loading ramp. He spun around, gunned it, and headed back just as the first of the Cycle Lords blocked the way out. Michael headed right for them, hunched over, looking hard at them through the visor of his black helmet. He saw the white eyes of two of them as he headed their way with several hundred pounds of steel.

Balmudo screamed, "Stop him!"

Michael fishtailed his bike, slapping the front wheels of two of the Cycle Lords around as he turned to race back down toward the dead end again.

"Got 'im!" a denimed biker cried.

A police car came up behind them, flashing lights and wailing its siren. Michael zipped down the alley, went clattering up the loading ramp . . . and into the air!

He went into the air with his front wheel turned because he knew he did not have much time or space in which to translate his forward motion into a sideways turn when he landed. He leaned to the left to compensate for the g-forces of the landing, and hit the asphalt beyond with a crash. He expected to go end over end into the parked cars beyond—but he didn't. His rear shocks were thumping as all the weight came down.

It was rough, but he wrenched the motorcycle erect and gunned it down the darkened street. He was more than a little surprised with himself.

"I did it," he said aloud. "Brando or McQueen couldn't have done it any better." A regular damned stuntman, he thought.

Up-up-and-away.

The lot was filled with chaos and confusion. The Cycle Lords raced around to attempt to get away from the police cars. A third and fourth car arrived, with one blocking an exit just as they all headed for it.

One of the police cars rocked from the impact of several heavy Harleys. Balmudo ordered them toward the south exit. They remounted their capsized machines and were off before the startled cops could get out of their cars.

Sirens wailed and cycles thundered.

Men screamed and horns honked.

The Cycle Lords slipped through the parked cars and into the street. They clattered along next to the police cars in the exits and made their escapes.

The police sirens wailed and the cars spun around, tires smoking, to give chase.

It was over in a moment. The lot was quiet. The neon lights flickered. Nogerilli's fingersnap sounded loudly.

"Everyone inside," he ordered. "We bowl."

They started drifting inside, half-listening to the fading thunder, discussing it in low tones. Only Rhonda, Paulette, Sharon, and Stephanie were left in the parking lot.

"Come on," Rhonda suggested.

"Count me out," Stephanie said absently to them.

"Hey," Paulette demanded, "what's eatin' *you*?"

"Nothin'," Stephanie said, making a gesture.

"You know, Steph, there's been talk," Sharon said.

Rhonda quickly interrupted her fellow Pink Lady. *"We* haven't been talkin' but Sharon's right. There's been talk . . . uh . . . questioning your loyalty to the T-birds, Steph."

"It doesn't mean you gotta go steady with Johnny," Paulette added. "In fact, uh, I think it's better for both of you that it's, you know, over."

Stephanie didn't say anything. She gazed out into the night beyond the brightly lit lot.

"But the code says we're T-bird chicks," Sharon said, "at least till grad."

Stephanie took a deep breath and blew it out sullenly. "Well . . . maybe I'm tired of being someone's chick."

"Tired of bein' someone's chick!" exclaimed Rhonda, shocked and surprised. "Are *you* feelin' okay?"

"I don't know what I'm feelin'," Stephanie answered honestly.

Paulette pulled out some cigarettes. "Here. Have a smoke. It'll make you feel much better."

Stephanie took the cigarette absently and put it in her lips. Paulette lit a match but, as Stephanie bent toward it, the flame flickered out in a gust of wind. She looked up and stopped.

A tall, backlit figure stood there—a man in black leather wearing a dark helmet with a closed visor. The machine, engine off, had coasted in while their attention was elsewhere. He stood there, outlined by his own headlight, with legs apart and cool. She stared as he flipped away the cigarette in his gloved hand and calmly turned to remount his machine. He kickstarted it deftly, revved the engine, then in one smooth motion started forward and reared up into a wheelie, riding on his back tire right up to the mesmerized Stephanie.

The cigarette was still between her lips. The rider stopped, pulled out a lighter, and held the flame out to her. She inhaled automatically, staring into the gleaming reflection in his dark visor.

"Want to ride?" he asked.

Stephanie opened her mouth, but a siren blared. A police car skidded into the parking lot and headed straight for the motorcyclist.

"Some other time," Michael said calmly. He popped his clutch and roared out of the lot with the police car screaming right past the stunned Pink Ladies.

Johnny Nogerilli stood inside with one hand on the cigarette machine. He had seen everything that had taken place in the lot and he was not pleased.

He saw the Pink Ladies turn and come chattering into the bowling alley, and he busied himself opening the package of smokes.

Something was going to have to be done, he thought.

☆ CHAPTER 12 ☆

Rhonda was bopping down the east corridor
of Rydell High when Goose McKenzie
caught up to her. He brought up an old argument.

"Why can't we just go to the drive-in and
make out like normal people, huh? I'm *tired*
of goin' to dumb dances every Saturday
night and gettin' stepped on."

Rhonda flipped her hair. "I need my
'National Bandstand' practice, that's why.
One more time."

"Jeez," Goose grumbled. He pulled a
ruler from his notebook and held it up to her
face like a handmike. "Name?"

"Rhonda Ritter, sixteen," she said in a
cute voice.

"How do you rate the record, Rhonda

Ritter?" Goose asked in as deep a voice as he could manage.

"It's pretty useless to dance to," she said after a second's judicious pause. "It's got pretty useless words. I give it a ninety-eight."

With a smile, she turned from Goose and headed toward a classroom, giving him a finger-waggling wave over her shoulder. She ran smack into an opening door. She collapsed back into Goose's arms with a gasp, holding her nose, verging on tears.

☆ ☆ ☆

The carrot made a loud crunching sound as Frenchy nibbled away at it. Michael sat next to her, munching a sandwich. They both stared at the Rube Goldberg-like apparatus spread out across a lab table. Bubbling, hissing, and dripping sounds prevailed.

Michael indicated the collection of tubes, condensers, and beakers with his sandwich. "What are you working on?"

"Joost cogmachtics . . ." She swallowed the carrot chunks and repeated herself. "Just cosmetics." Then abruptly she turned to Michael to whisper excitedly. "Michael, I heard there was this motorcycle chase outside the Bowl-A-Rama last night, and . . ."

she took a deep breath. "According to Paulette Rebcheck, who shall go nameless except here, this very mysterious and *gorgeous* guy knocked one Stephanie Zinone right out of her bobby socks. How do you plead?"

He hesitated, then grinned. "Guilty."

"I knew it!" she exclaimed and grabbed him around the neck. "Oh, wow, *wow!*"

"Yeah," Michael said. "But now what?"

"It worked," she said with conviction. "That's the good news. The *bad* news is that Johnny Nogerilli is reported to be *very* jealous, and he wants to turn this guy's face into cream of wheat."

"Which is my face," Michael said gloomily, looking at his sandwich.

"You got it," Frenchy said. "So be careful."

Michael shrugged. "I . . . I can handle them. It's Stephanie who's the problem." He peered at his sandwich as if the answer lay in the chicken salad. "She's got me completely confused. I was never confused about anything like this at home. . . ." He looked up at Frenchy and smiled crookedly. "But then there was no Miss Stephanie Zinone at home. There was Elizabeth Dempsey," he admitted. "Elizabeth liked me for who I was. . . ."

"But?" Frenchy prompted.

"But Elizabeth also liked to spend our Saturday nights stuffing insects for biology class."

"That sounds interesting," Frenchy admitted wryly.

"Stuffed insects have their romantic limitations, Frenchy."

"I know what you mean," she shivered. "Insects give me the creeps. Too many legs, too shiny or squishy. . . ."

"But with Elizabeth," Michael continued, "at least I had only one life to lead. Here," he gestured, "I'm leading two."

"Which beats stuffing ants," Frenchy suggested.

Michael nodded. "On that cycle, I knocked her out of her socks, but like this, I . . ." He gestured to indicate his present condition.

"Knock her *into* her socks," Frenchy suggested.

"I'm going to tell her," Michael said with sudden determination.

Frenchy sighed. "I guess a man's gotta do what a man's gotta do."

Michael was paying no attention to her mild irony. "It's simple," he explained to himself. "I have to tell her the next time I see her."

"Oh!" Frenchy said. She saw all of the Pink Ladies coming through the lab door.

And Rhonda had a big bandage across her nose.

But Michael had not yet noticed the newcomers. "I'm going to walk right up to her," he vowed, "and—"

"Hi, you guys!" Frenchy said loudly, giving Michael a quick look.

He turned and saw all of them and swallowed. Sharon sauntered up, looking at the bubbling glass pots. "Getting a facial?" she asked Michael, getting a laugh from the others even though Rhonda's laugh ended in a grimace.

Michael looked at Stephanie and felt very strange inside. He said her name in a rather odd voice.

"Yeah?" Stephanie responded, eyeing the collection of tubes and flasks.

"Have you ever stuffed an insect?" Michael asked.

She looked at her watch. "Not in the last few hours."

"Just checking," Michael said and abruptly left.

Rhonda raised her eyebrows. "That boy needs a guidance counselor." She saw him pass Nogerilli in the hallway and saw the T-bird leader's cold stare.

"Rhonda!" Frenchy exclaimed. "You got a nose job!"

"Forget it," she grumbled. "I walked

into a door. That klutz Bruce Sanders just charged right out."

"Into a *door*?" Frenchy said, almost laughing, but trying to control herself.

"So *she* says," Sharon said, checking the levelness of her pillbox hat.

Paulette poked Frenchy's arm. "Stephanie wants the complete treatment—eyes, nails, the works."

Frenchy smiled. "What's the occasion, Steph?"

The blonde shrugged casually. "It's no big occasion."

Paulette pushed her. "Much. It's the guy from the Bowl-A-Rama, who is just about the sexiest thing I've ever seen . . . outside of Johnny Nogerilli, that is."

Frenchy took Stephanie's arm and turned her toward the light. "Um," she said, examining the field of work. "Um. Umm."

"Stop 'umming' and start strumming," Sharon said.

"Then let's start with the eyes," Frenchy said in a professional tone. "The eyes are the doors to the heart and mind and the eye-shadow is the doormat."

"Whatever you say," Stephanie said. She sat on the indicated stool, and Frenchy got out her box of makeup gear. The Pink Ladies gathered about, eager to learn any of the many crafts and skills needed for perfection.

Stephanie caught a glimpse of herself, somewhat distorted, in a reflection from a polished hubcap, then she slid under the 1958 Dodge in her father's garage with a crescent wrench in her hand.

Too much makeup for a grease monkey, she thought. It's like a debutante in pearls slinging hash. She angrily attacked the shocks on the car, her wrench clanging.

She heard a motorcycle approach and stop outside by the gas pumps. The customer bell rang as he rolled to a stop. Stephanie grumbled as she slid out and tossed the wrench into the top of the big red tool case where it spun around noisily. She snatched at an oily rag on a barrel of thirty-weight oil and scrubbed her hands. You never *really* get the grease out from under your fingernails, she thought.

Without looking at the customer—just another biker in standard leathers, she thought—she hefted the gas hose and reached for the tank top. "Fill it up?" she asked automatically and heard an assenting grunt. Another car drove in, crunching on

133

the gravel and honking its horn from beyond the other pump.

Stephanie gave the car a dark look and muttered to herself. "No one shows up for an hour, then everyone decides they need gas at once. Okay, okay," she said loudly, aiming her complaint at the car. "Keep your shirt on."

She hung up the hose, looked at the indicator, and started putting his gas cap back on. "That'll be one-sixty," she said.

The biker held out the money. "Want that ride now?" Michael asked.

Her head snapped up. It was *his* voice! "You!"

He nodded, the sun reflecting off his dark visor. "Uh-huh."

The waiting car honked again, but Stephanie just stared, unable to see the face behind the dark plastic. The impatient driver leaned on the horn for a long blast, then another car turned off the street and came up to Michael's motorcycle.

"Hold on!" Stephanie yelled at the first driver. "I—"

"Hey, sweetheart," the first driver yelled. "Fill her up and check the oil." Stephanie heard him say something to his wife. "If she can find the hood. Women mechanics, jeez!"

The second driver stuck his head out of

the window of his 1950 Chevy pickup. "What's the story here?"

Stephanie tore her gaze away from the tall biker and stepped angrily to the window of the first car. She grasped the door and snarled into the car. "Honk that horn where the sun don't shine!"

The driver almost jumped into his wife's lap. He stared at the angry girl as she stomped over to the cycle, tossed her oily rag on the ground, and swung her coveralled legs onto it, grasping the masked biker around the waist. Without a word, Michael stood on the starter and the cycle thundered to life. They gunned out of the gas station, spitting gravel, and raced away.

The honking horns behind them faded and the last thing Stephanie heard was one of them saying, "But I'm almost out . . ."

They rode for hours until they stopped to watch the setting sun. It gleamed on the biker's dark helmet as Stephanie raised her face to his. His lips were warm and firm just below the face mask that darkened his features.

They kissed, long and hard.

Stephanie's body quivered slightly. When they broke apart she gasped, "I . . . I can't stop shivering."

The biker smiled and turned around to fire up his machine. "Then hold on," he said.

135

"That's what's making me shiver," Stephanie said, grabbing the nameless, faceless young man around the waist and burying her head against his back. She shivered with her eyes closed as they bumped onto the asphalt, picking up speed.

It was early evening when they got back to the station. She felt pangs of guilt. She had run off and left it unattended, the cash register open, Mrs. Jumper's car shocks still unfixed, tools left out. The lights weren't even on.

But the guilt was washed over by a feeling of . . . of what? she asked herself. Fulfillment? Pleasure? Stolen sweets? The realization of a dimly understood twist of fate? Whatever it was, she thought, the gas station was less important than what happened this afternoon.

When the motorcycle stopped, she stayed hugging against his jacket. She didn't want the moment to end. The bike would turn into a pumpkin, her ball gown back into greasy overalls.

She opened her eyes and lifted her face as the man she was holding turned. They kissed, long and soft and sweet, just as if they knew all about each other.

Am I in love? she asked herself.

And who *is* this guy?

Neither of them noticed Nogerilli, Dimucci, and Davey cruise by and stop. Paulette, Rhonda, and Sharon were on the backs of their bikes. They saw the cycle in the shadows and automatically looked.

"Check *this* out," Dimucci said, seeing the couple kiss.

Nogerilli glowered for a moment, then gunned his engine. "Let's go," he said. They took off, swinging back onto the street and disappearing into the night.

In the dimness of the gas station's yard, the young biker and Stephanie nuzzled happily. Then the biker took a deep breath and shoved up his visor. Stephanie looked at him, but the shadows were too deep, too dark. He was just a shape.

"There's . . . there's something I think I should tell you," Michael said.

"What?"

Then he heard the returning motorcycles and looked up to see their headlights bobbing toward him. "Oh, no," he groaned. He pulled his visor back down. "We've got company," he said.

Stephanie stepped off the bike and looked back, but her head snapped around as she heard him kickstart his motorcycle. "No, wait!" she said. "Don't go. I can handle this!"

He looked at her over his shoulder. "Crowds make me nervous."

He revved the engine and wheeled the bike around. "Wait!" Stephanie yelled over the noise. "When will I see—"

"Friday!" he yelled, banging in the clutch and taking off. "The talent show! Out front!"

He made a fancy, daring wheelie that scattered gravel as he shot out of the gas station. Stephanie put out a hand toward him. "Hey, wait! How do you know about—"

But he was gone. She stood in the middle of the drive, staring after him, her thoughts and emotions in a turmoil.

The T-birds roared in and stopped just behind her. "Hey," Nogerilli said, "what's the story with the creep on the bike, Zinone?"

Stephanie was still looking at the empty street where the faceless, nameless biker had disappeared. "What?" she said vaguely.

"The story!" Nogerilli growled. "The *creep!*"

"Yeah," Goose added. "That creep! The whole story, huh?"

Rhonda slapped his shoulder. "Shut up, Goose."

"Leave her be, Johnny," Paulette said softly, with a bitter edge to her voice.

Nogerilli shot a few words over his shoulder to Paulette. "You shut up." To Stephanie he said, "Let's have it!"

Stephanie turned slowly, her thoughts elsewhere. "Have what?"

"The *story!*" Nogerilli said impatiently.

Sharon spoke up, "Personally, I think—"

Davey and Dimucci spoke together. "We don't *care*, Sharon!"

Nogerilli made an impatient gesture. "Everyone, shut *up!* Listen, Zinone, no chick of mine messes with no other creep except me!"

Paulette looked indignant. "No chick of *yours?*"

"Someone's jealous," Sharon sing-songed.

Paulette said angrily, "Yeah, well, why don't you get jealous like that over me, John Nogerilli?"

"Because I *ain't* jealous!" he growled.

Stephanie became aware of him at last. "Then stay out of my life, Johnny." She turned and walked into the gas station to close it up for the night.

"I'm out," Nogerilli called. "But if I see you with that punk one more time, he's a dead man."

Paulette's chin quivered and the tears came quickly. "Look J-Johnny, you b-better decide once and f-for all w-w-who belongs to who around here."

Nogerilli frowned and said in a low voice, "You're makin' a scene, Paulette."

"And I'm gettin' pretty mixed up, too," she said with her voice quavering. "And I don't like how that feels one bit."

Furiously, she jumped off the motorcycle and ran across the gravel to the mechanic's bay, where Stephanie put an arm around her, patting her shoulder. Sharon and Rhonda got off, too, and walked over to comfort their friend.

Sharon snapped at Nogerilli, "I think you owe Paulette an apology."

"Jerk," Rhonda said nastily.

Davey shook his head. "Weirdos."

"Who needs broads?" Goose sighed.

Dimucci spoke up. "Me! I get to second base with Sharon and keep gettin' called out when I try to steal third."

Goose laughed. "Poor boy bombed out in the bomb shelter."

"I think we all need a little guaranteed action . . . and I know *just* the place," Nogerilli leered.

☆CHAPTER 13☆

Yvette Mason's well-made-up mouth was pursed as she leafed through the essays on her desk. She looked around suspiciously. "There is some very good work here. Maybe a little *too* good." Her eyes swept the class again. "Suspiciously good." She saw self-satisfied smiles on the faces of Nogerilli and McKenzie. "There's also some very sloppy work here." She was about to continue when the bell rang.

All the students jumped up and started gathering books, but Miss Mason's voice sang out over the noise. "Miss Zinone . . . I want to talk to you about your Shakespeare essay."

After a few minutes, Stephanie emerged with her essay. "Shakespeare!" she muttered to herself. "Who asked him to write all that stuff any—"

She hadn't seen Michael and ran right into him. "—way!" She looked up at him with mild impatience, then just stepped around him and walked on. Michael followed her and caught up.

"I guess Miss Mason didn't like your paper, huh?"

"To say the least," she grumbled. "I gotta do it *all* over again."

"Want some help?"

"Help?" she asked, frowning. "I don't know."

"Well, ol' Bill and I, we're both Englishmen, y'know. Well, think it over. It's not a difficult decision."

Paulette and Sharon were closing their lockers as Michael and Stephanie passed. "Steph, you comin'?" Paulette called out.

Stephanie stopped and turned back to her friends. She looked over her shoulder at Michael, who had also stopped. "I'll think about it," she said, giving him a quick and rather polite smile.

Michael watched them go on down the hall, heads together.

Ray's Diner was not exactly the best eating spot in town, but the booth tables were big enough and no one minded a couple of kids spreading out their homework. Stephanie looked at her hamburger and glanced around to catch the eye of the waitress.

"Know the first rule of waitressing?" she asked Michael, who shook his head. "Once you have served a customer you never look at them again. If you do pay attention, it is only to ask if everything is all right when their mouth is full."

Michael laughed and looked around for the waitress, too. Some truckers and an older couple were having coffee at the counter.

Stephanie turned back to her homework and jabbed a finger at her essay. "You know what Hamlet's big problem is?"

"What?" Michael asked.

"No ketchup." She turned to seek out the waitress again.

"He seemed to get along pretty well without it," he said.

"I don't usually do this bad in English," she said. "It's just that . . . well, I got other things on my mind these days."

"Anything I can help you with?" he asked.

She pointed at another booth. "Yeah, shoot that ketchup over here, huh?"

He got it and handed it over. "There's something I think I should tell you, Stephanie," he began.

"It's this guy," she said, squirting on the red stuff.

"What guy?" Michael was somewhat taken aback.

She slapped on the top half of the bun and took a big bite, chewing it and offering the hamburger to Michael, who shook his head. "The other thing on my mind," she explained. "See, the crazy thing is I've seen him twice and both times he's wearin' this visor." She made a gesture and a drop of ketchup splattered on the table. "I don't even know what he looks like or who he is or anything!"

Michael cleared his throat. "Ah . . . I think there's something I should tell you. . . ."

Stephanie took a huge bite out of the hamburger and the ketchup oozed out. "That's better," she said in satisfaction, inspecting the remains of the sandwich. "How can you eat a hamburger without ketchup?" she asked him. "Bite?"

"No, thanks," he said, shaking his head again. "Look, I—"

"Yeah, well, what's bothering me is maybe this Mister Right isn't everything I've built up in my mind. Maybe behind that

144

visor is just some ordinary . . ." She waved the hamburger around, looking for the right word.

Michael lost his nerve. He reached for her essay. "Maybe we should look at your essay."

"Oh, yeah," she said, shoving it toward him. "Read this."

Michael opened it and started reading. He raised his eyes to Stephanie, who winced.

"Not so hot, huh?"

"You seem to have the right idea," he said carefully.

"Yeah?" she brightened.

"But you might have said, 'Hamlet was tormented by his mother's infidelity'".

Stephanie set the half-eaten sandwich down and snatched up a pen. Infidelity. "Oh, God, Mason's gonna flip when she reads this." She looked up at him quickly. "You must think I'm some kinda dummy, right?"

He paused, then just plunged ahead. "Actually, I think you're kind of terrific."

"Get out," she said, waving her pen at him. *"You're* the terrific one. I mean," she said, gesturing across the table at all the books and notebooks, "you understand all this deep junk and everything."

He smiled faintly. "I don't understand all that deep junk any better than you. I just know a few big words . . . or maybe just *acceptable* words."

"Well, it impresses the hell out of me," she said. She resumed writing. "And I give credit to who I want, okay?"

"To whom," he corrected.

"Who . . . whom," she said with a dismissive gesture. "Learn how to take a compliment, okay?"

"Okay," he said.

"And lighten up."

"Okay," he agreed.

"And eat those fries and stop saying 'okay.'"

"Oh . . . all right," he said, correcting himself. "You know . . . you're the most beautiful girl I've ever—"

But she hadn't heard him. "I think we've got this essay licked," she said with satisfaction. "I'll just put in big teacher-type words for my street words, right?" A waitress passed and Stephanie waved at her. "A burger for my friend here. Loaded," she added.

Michael sighed and looked at the ketchup bottle suspiciously.

Nogerilli and Goose parked their bikes on the side of Ray's Diner, just beneath a billboard advertising the new Marilyn Monroe movie.

Goose looked up at the billboard and licked his lips. "Paulette will havta see that one," he said, but Nogerilli wasn't listening.

"There are some very cool broads who hang out at this joint," he said, trying to see through the reflections in the windows.

Goose let out an excited cry and said, "Just like at the supermarket?"

They swaggered toward the corner. Then Nogerilli grabbed Goose and pulled him back against the Coca Cola sign. "Shut up!" Goose looked around and saw Michael Carrington and Stephanie emerge from the diner. The T-birds can hear but are not noticed by the two they are watching.

Stephanie pulled on her jacket. "You know, I've been thinkin'," she said. "I bet there's a million girls who'd love to go out with someone like you."

Michael said, "What about you?"

"*Me*?" She looked at him as if his hair was on fire. "Are you *kidding*?"

Michael stared at her and couldn't conceal his hurt. He turned to go, yanking on his jacket. Stephanie realized she had inadvertently made a terrible goof. She took a few steps toward him. "Hey, uh, I didn't mean it that way." She made a gesture of indecision. "We're, ah, we're just different types, that's all."

Michael kept walking, ignoring her. She read the hurt in his hunched shoulders. She watched him walk off and tried to think of something to say but couldn't.

There's this guy . . . .

He's all I ever wanted and . . . .

What was the use? she thought. Guys were always so huffy when you turn them down. But I didn't mean to hurt him, she thought. He's a nice guy and if he found the right woman he'd be super . . . but . . .

"Anyway," she yelled after him, "There's, like, you know, a Pink Lady code . . . ." She realized that was not a very convincing reason. Michael stopped and looked back.

"Well, to quote Dolores," he said, "the code stinks." He turned and walked away.

After a few seconds, Stephanie hugged her books to her and turned to walk the other way. She bumped right into Goose and Nogerilli as they sauntered around the corner.

"What's this?" Goose said, pointing toward the retreating Michael, "noids night out?"

"You a cop?" demanded Stephanie. Goose's eyebrows went up. She started to step past them and Nogerilli grabbed her arm.

148

"You sure have picked up lots of new friends, Zinone," he said. "I guess the T-birds ain't the class act no more, huh?"

"Yeah," Goose sneered, "I guess we ain't got no class no more, huh?"

Nogerilli gave Goose a dark look. "Shut your face and wait inside."

"Aw, I don't wanna eat alone, Johnny," Goose complained.

"Go!" Nogerilli ordered, pointing.

"Okay, okay," Goose grumbled to him. "Jeez . . . ."

Stephanie said, "Why don't you guys mind your own business?"

"You *are* my business," Nogerilli said with menace.

Stephanie made a show of annoyance. "What do you want, Johnny?"

"I am officially declarin' us as an item officially over," he announced.

"*You're* declarin'?" she frowned.

"That's correct," he said with dignity.

"Fine," she said, waving her hand. "You've declared. It's over." She looked wryly at him and paused. "Can I go now?"

He nodded curtly, then held up a hand. "One last thing. That jacket's T-bird property. You wanna leave the party, drop the jacket at the door on your way out." He sniffed. "We got a rep to protect. Don't mess with the rep, we won't mess with your new friends. Dig?"

Stephanie just looked at him, then walked off without a word. Nogerilli watched her walk away, then turned with great nonchalance to saunter over to where Goose was waiting by the door of the diner.

Goose shook his head sadly. "So she took the noid's brains over your brawns, Johnny."

Nogerilli exploded in anger, grabbing Goose's throat in a tight squeeze. Goose's mouth dropped open and his eyes popped in fear. He made no motion to protect himself. He and Johnny had fought it out a long time before. They each knew who would win.

"*I* dumped *her*!" Johnny snarled angrily. "Not versa visa! Got it?"

"Yeah," Goose choked. "Sure . . . *yeow*, Johnny . . . uh . . ."

Nogerilli removed his fingers from Goose's throat, but for a long time Goose could feel those strong hands choking him, cutting off the blood and air.

Michael went into the cafeteria and saw Stephanie well up in line, near the milk. He worked his way into the line and squeezed past several students, all of whom protested or gave him angry glares. But the young exchange student just ignored the protests and muttered, "Excuse me?" as he moved along until he could get into line directly ahead of Stephanie.

She didn't notice him put his tray down on the stainless steel rods ahead of her. She was concentrating on deciding between skim milk or coffee. At the sudden burst of noise, she did look around just as the T-birds came bursting into the cafeteria in their usual noisy way.

They were supporting a stricken-looking Goose, who was bug-eyed, waving spread fingers at the counter and crying out, "Food! Food! *Food!*"

The T-birds bullied their way into the line, but no one did anything more than look disgusted or sullen. The leather-jacketed quartet shoved rudely at people, and one of those bumped back into Stephanie.

The girl stumbled and grabbed at Michael's leather-coated back, her face shoved against him.

I've been here before, she thought. But when?

Michael turned his head and looked down at her as she recovered her balance. "Hi," he said.

"Hi," she said, smiling and then nervously letting it fade away. "Uh . . ." she said, indicating the noisy group a few feet behind her. Michael nodded.

Stephanie grabbed a wrapped sandwich and hurried through the line, paying as quickly as possible and almost fleeing to a table.

What was that about? she wondered. It seemed familiar to her and vaguely pleasant.

She concentrated on unwrapping the sandwich. Ham and Cheese. *Damn!* She hated cheese in sandwiches. They always used the cheap kind. But she had grabbed the first one within reach because something was happening . . . but what?

Michael stood holding his tray, watching Stephanie unwrap her sandwich. He felt foolish.

All dressed up, he thought, and no place to go. Just pretending I'm not who I am. He shook his head and took an indecisive step toward her. I'm really screwed up, he said to himself. By trying to be two people . . . but they both have the same heart.

He saw Stephanie bite angrily into her sandwich, staring off into space. She swallowed it in big bites, gulping down her milk. Why can't I just be whatever it is I am, he thought, and not hide behind some false image, an image she wants.

He took another hesitant step toward her, then saw her stare at the sandwich in apparent disgust. She wadded up the remains in the wrapper, gulped down the rest of the milk, and got up to stalk off.

Why can't she see that other me is just some kind of costume on wheels, he thought wearily. Stephanie stuffed the remains of her lunch in the trash and left the cafeteria with Paulette, who had just walked in.

Michael sighed and sat down at the nearest table, almost unaware that Sharon and Rhonda were there, finishing up, chattering about "Father Knows Best" and some ghost story on "The Twilight Zone." They finished and left.

Michael sat there, barely aware he was eating and totally unaware of what it was. Lies, he thought. Charades. They hide the real me, the me deep inside. Dumb posturing meant to disguise all the love I keep inside me.

The cafeteria slowly cleared out. There were only the sounds of the kitchen crew cleaning up. But can't she *feel* the real me? he thought. Behind this facade of lies. "Behind my charades," he said softly.

Michael walked into the empty auditorium and onto the stage. He sat down at the piano and began playing the song that had been running through his head. It was a song about lies and deceptions, even in the best of interests. A song about himself and Stephanie, but names were never mentioned. See the real me, the song pleaded. Behind the image, behind the smoke and dreams.

But, he wondered, had tne image, the bike rider, taken over and become the real me?

Had it?

☆CHAPTER 14☆

The T-birds swaggered up to the crowd around the bulletin board. Goose and Dimucci formed a flying wedge to push everyone back so that Nogerilli could walk up and read the "Talent Show Entries" list unobstructed.

Davey squinted close. "Disaster!" he announced.

"We blew it?" Goose said.

"No, we made it," Davey said. He looked at his friends. "But, we're the worst. We can't sing in *public*."

"Then we'll get unworst," Nogerilli announced like a true leader.

"We'll get liverworst," Goose said gloomily as they backed away from the bulletin board.

Davey was sick about it. "How did we get in?"

Dimucci gave him a quick grin. "Obviously, they recognize natural talent."

"Everyone got in," Eugene said, sticking his head into the group. "They didn't have enough acts."

The T-birds groaned.

☆   ☆   ☆

The smoke from their cigarettes was mingling with the steam from the nearby showers as the T-birds had an illegal smoke and wondered what they were going to do.

Nogerilli whispered, "If we're gonna land the grand prize—"

"Which is one hundred long playin' albumins," Goose inserted.

"We gotta get it together just like that buncha Preptones but with class."

They listened a moment, hearing the four singers in the showers smoothly sing a number called "Yellow Bird."

"Ech," Goose said.

"Milk," Dimucci said.

"But smooth, ya gotta admit," Davey said.

They looked at Nogerilli. He had that expression on his face, the "I'm Thinking" expression.

☆ ☆ ☆

The art department had made up a big banner: ANNUAL TALENT SHOW. It was draped across the entrance to Rydell High. Kids were arriving by car and on foot, parking down the street or in the parking lot, and coming in dressed up and slicked down. Skirts rustled around ankles. High heels made more than one young woman totter. Lipstick and hairspray. Perfume and nail polish.

Ties, jackets, slacks, cheeks scraped of scant growth, and a half-hour of haircombing. Masculine shaving lotion and clean shorts.

Stephanie paced nervously back and forth at the curb, impatient and rather jerky, barely acknowledging the greetings of her classmates, even the whistles and wolf calls. She looked unexpectedly feminine, especially to herself. The dress was bought last spring, the one she thought she'd never need. She wore *Evening in Paris*, even her mother's best pale rose nail polish.

"Evening, Stephanie," a voice called.

She turned to see Mr. Stuart approaching, his white teeth gleaming. Yvette Mason was with him sporting a well-sprayed hairdo, all smiles and crinoline. They were walking in with Mr. and Mrs. Tom Anderson.

Mrs. Anderson said, "I'm really happy for Michael. He seems to have fit in so well. He really loves it here."

Tom Anderson grinned and stuck out his chest proudly. "That's America, Helen. They don't call it the land of the free, the home of the brave for nothing."

Stephanie nodded briskly to Mr. Stuart, well aware that he had stripped her naked with one lecherous look.

Where *were* the girls? she wondered. And where is *he*?

Rhonda was driving her parents' car, with Paulette next to her, trying to put on lipstick to the rhythm of the potholes in the street. In the back, little Dolores sat next to Sharon, who was brushing her hair.

Dolores looked from one to the other, observing how they went through the ritual. You never know when you are going to need these skills, she thought. But they *are* a little overdressed, she thought. Or is it just that I'm so used to seeing them in T-bird jackets and tight slacks that anything with a skirt makes them look like "Gone With The Wind" extras?

"She said he's going to meet her out front," Paulette said.

"She just wants us for moral support," Dolores said.

"How anyone can get so hot over some-one she doesn't even know," Sharon grumbled, whipping the brush through her hair, "is *totally* beyond me."

Dolores sighed. Growing up had all sorts of complications she had never imagined. Too bad you couldn't just freeze yourself at some point and stay that age.

Stephanie heard the motorcycle sounds and her blonde head went up. She flipped away the cigarette that she had been nervously puffing and looked up the street.

The T-birds were approaching, elegant in their special gold lamé sports coats, glittering on their shining machines. From the other direction, she heard another motorcycle and her head snapped around to see the tall rider in his dark helmet and black leather.

Him!

The T-birds saw him, too. Goose's hand went out. "Johnny! It's that guy!"

The T-bird leader's jaw tightened. "This time," he said in a harsh voice, "we nail him."

Their engines roared almost as one and they leaped ahead, scattering well-dressed students and a few outraged parents.

"Look out!" Stephanie cried.

The faceless rider gunned his own engine and shot straight at the approaching T-birds. As he passed Stephanie, he called out, "I'll be back!"

The startled T-birds parted before him and he shot through. They spun around, muscling their 600-pound Harleys roughly, making the switch in direction.

Nogerilli paused, looking hard at Stephanie. "This time," he called to her and made a gesture across his throat.

"No!" she shouted, frightened for him. "Johnny!"

The bikers roared back down the street, just missing Tom Anderson. "Damn subversive commie bikers!" he yelled at them.

The Pink Ladies drove up and Stephanie waved them down before they turned off into the parking lot. Rhonda hit the accelerator pedal and jumped toward the wild-eyed Stephanie. The door flew open and Stephanie climbed in next to Paulette as the car moved.

"Go!" she shouted. "They're going to kill him!"

Sharon stepped on the gas pedal and the old Ford picked up speed. "We're going to be late," she said grimly.

Dolores leaned over from the rear. "Step on it!"

The bikes roared up the twisting hillside road. Michael's bike cut the inside curve, squashed a Budweiser can flat with a pop, and tooled around the sharp curve.

Four motorcycles were not far behind.

Behind them, Rhonda fought the bad shocks in the old Ford, which made the car tilt on the curves. They careened off into the gravel of the shoulder and all the women screamed, but Rhonda fought it back onto the road.

"Oh, my God!" Sharon groaned.

Rhonda was frantically searching the street ahead, trying to see what had caused Sharon to yell. Was it a child in the road? A dead body? A dumped bike? A truck? "*What?*" she yelled back.

"We're going to die," moaned Sharon, "and I'm wearing my mother's underwear!"

"The Penny stuff or the Frederick's of Hollywood stuff?" Dolores asked.

Michael's bike roared up the curving street. The domes and arches of the Griffith Park Observatory were ahead, much higher on the hill, bringing him quick visions of Jimmy Dean and "Rebel Without a Cause" and old Flash Gordon serials.

Then the road branched—one up, one down. He went down, not seeing the ROAD CLOSED sign tipped over by the wind.

Down and out the other side, he thought. Away from these guys, back to Stephanie, back to—what? To tell her who I really am!

The construction barriers came up fast. The T-birds were coming up behind him. There was a loading ramp for the bulldozer parked off to the side.

He didn't hesitate. Up the ramp and out—into the darkness beyond—he went.

The T-birds braked and slid to a stop before the barriers. There was a cliff just off the shoulder, a steep drop through chaparral and cactus, which none of them wanted to experience, especially astride a heavy Harley going end over end.

"Jeez," Davey said, shaking his head, looking into the darkness beyond their lights. "I figured the guy would slow up. Right, Johnny?"

Dimucci spoke. "Yeah. It ain't our fault the guy didn't slow up, right, Johnny?"

Goose grinned. "You want us to walk down and view the remains?"

Nogerilli was hanging tough, but he wasn't really feeling all that tough. "Da guy is hiss-tow-ree," he shrugged. "So leave us not cry over spilled grease."

Goose was trying to emulate Johnny's toughness, but the thought that they might be held responsible for the mystery rider's death made him nervous. "Yeah," he agreed. "Hiss-tow-ree."

Their heads snapped around as they heard the squealing tires of an approaching car. They saw it appear, brake, and go into a long slide of considerable noise, heading right for them. They almost had to jump over the cliff to escape the onrushing vehicle.

Before the car even stalled out, Stephanie had jumped from it and ran gasping over to the cliff to look down into the dark. "Where is he?" she cried out hysterically.

The other Pink Ladies tumbled from the car and grabbed her. Dimucci shook his head. "He ain't down there!"

Nogerilli looked around with a knowing grin on his face. "Where'd he go, huh, heaven?"

The T-birds laughed, but it was a nervous laugh indeed. Goose spoke up, covering his nervousness with a judicious air. "I figure the only thing possible is when he hit the ramp, he went over and kept goin'."

There was a short silence. Nogerilli said quietly, looking at the distraught Stephanie, "Let's get outta here."

They climbed on their machines and kicked them alive, taking off one by one at a medium speed.

The sound of their engines faded down the hillside. The night was quiet except for Stephanie's short, sad sobs.

"What have I done?" she said to herself.

Paulette tugged at her arm. "Steph,

don't worry. He'll be okay. He's the rider. Come on, you can't stay here."

Sharon took Stephanie's other arm, pulling her toward the car. "Come on, let's go back."

The crying blonde let herself be put into the car, but she stared straight ahead, with tears creeping down her cheeks.

CHAPTER 15

A tall skinny kid in an oversized sports jacket and a loud tie was doing a Johnny Ray impression. He cried and ripped at his shirt as he sang "Cry," standing before the auditorium curtain.

Paulette came stamping down from the dressing rooms in a scanty bikini, which beautifully showed off her lush, young body. Nogerilli, dirty and tattered from the cycle trip, was angrily waving his hands right behind her. "You're not goin' out there like *that!*" he proclaimed.

"I know," she agreed. "I've gotta put something on my face."

"You gotta put a little something on your *body!*" he announced. He grabbed her and pulled her toward the shadows, shielding her body from the curious.

"I *gotta* dress like this, Johnny," she explained. "I'm summer."

He shook her a little. "Then get a pair of galoshes and a snowsuit and be winter!" He released her abruptly and straightened up. "And *that* is my last word!"

Paulette stopped being polite. She stopped being diplomatic. She stopped being apologetic. "Well, you wanna hear my last word, Mister Push-Everyone-Around Nogerilli?"

It was obvious that he didn't, and he liked even less the finger she jabbed into his chest. "Maybe you can bully most of the kids in this school, but *this* kid's been bullied for the last time." She jabbed him in the chest again, and he stepped back. The worm had turned. The natives were revolting.

"I may not be the classiest chick around," she snapped, "but I'm as good as you are gonna get, John Nogerilli." She jabbed him in the chest and he backed up. "So take it or *leave* it!"

The last jab shoved Nogerilli right through the center opening of the auditorium curtain. There was a gasp from the people sitting out front heard even over the singer's sobs. Nogerilli looked down to see the singing, weeping, shouting, crying creature on his knees just before him, tearing himself apart in amorous anguish.

The singer saw Nogerilli and just automatically incorporated him into the act. He grabbed at the T-bird's dark trousers, still singing "Cry" at the top of his adolescent lungs. Nogerilli was confused and embarrassed and made getaway motions with his hand. He heard the worst thing a T-bird can hear—a snicker.

"Hey! Get offa me! Hey!" Nogerilli waggled a leg, trying to free his limb and escape into the blissful darkness of backstage. He bent over and snarled into the sobbing youth's ear, "Leggo or I'll bust ya face!"

Without missing a beat, the singer threw out his arms, and Nogerilli stomped off the stage, flushed and angry. The "Johnny Ray" singer finished to big applause.

Nogerilli waved to Davey, Dimucci, and Goose with an abrupt gesture. Stiffly, he marched away, saying, "Let's go practice up in the can."

"What was that?" Goose asked, aiming a thumb over his shoulder at the stage. "You got a special act goin' or somethin'?"

"Shut up."

Miss McGee checked her schedule. "And now, Martin Miesner and his red-hot accordian!"

The accordian player began playing "Lady of Spain." Two sophomores, rather shabbily dressed in Spanish costumes, danced around until the number was finished and Miss McGee came out to thank them.

The T-birds emerged from the shower stalls, combing their hair and looking doubtful. But there was no doubt in Nogerilli's voice. "That takes care of the competition," he snapped. "Let's move it." He gave the direction with a sharp gesture of his forefinger.

The T-birds trooped out of the bathroom, and for several seconds there was silence. Then the muffled groans and fruitless struggles of the four Preptones, in their very best costumes, tied and gagged, could be faintly heard from beneath the cascading showers.

"We're goin' prowlin'," the T-birds sang on stage, grinning out at the auditorium of parents, teachers, and students.

"Walk, talk like a T-bird!"

Backstage, Rhonda had a firm grip on Stephanie's arm, pulling her toward the calendar girl set with fierce determina-

168

tion, although there were still tears on Stephanie's face.

"We *need* you!" Rhonda argued.

"I can't," Stephanie sobbed, "I just *can't!*

She looked up and blinked through her tears as Michael came around the set and into their path. He was tying his tie and wearing a sports jacket over his jeans. "Wait," he said, putting out a hand. "I want to talk to you."

But Stephanie would have none of it. "Get away from me!" she said angrily, another sob racking her body.

Her sobs were smothered by the applause from the audience as the T-birds finished their number. They raced off the stage, grinning like fools, elated and bouncing, running past McGee.

The principal stepped out from behind the curtain, saying, "The T-bones."

"Birds!" Nogerilli shouted. *"Birds!"*

Miss McGee was a bit confused, but she consulted her schedule and went doggedly on. "And now, let's hear it for the calendar girls." The curtains parted and revealed the spring-summer-fall-winter decor and all of the girls in their appropriate costumes.

Stephanie was trying to control herself and hoped the tears could not be seen by the audience. The words came and her mouth moved, but she wasn't really singing along with the rest. Every line stabbed into her like a dagger. Every vow to be true, to be one-and-only, to love and hold and be faithful, drove a spike into her mind.

Then it was her cue. Her moment. Her solo.

There was a short pause and Sharon's face contorted. It was winter's cue, but Stephanie hadn't picked it up. The other girls looked at her and saw her mouth moving, but heard no sound. The girls all prodded her on, whispering the first line, urging her to start. But she couldn't.

The audience had perceived Stephanie's predicament by this time and had begun to "Aaaaah" and "Ooooo" sympathetically. The musicians faltered.

"I'm sorry," Stephanie said in a hoarse whisper. "I . . . I c-can't . . ."

From the catwalk, Eugene called down in a stage whisper, "What about the snow?"

Sharon gave up.

For Stephanie, the moment seemed to last forever. The acute embarrassment, the pain, the frustration, the sadness all stretched out. Her eyes misted and she dreamed . . .

It was her lover's last ride . . .

Over the ramp . . .

Up into the darkness and beyond . . .

Into Biker Heaven . . .

He was surrounded by T-birds and Pink Ladies, all smooth and sleek and cool. The vision was slightly blurred, as if everything had been airbrushed to perfection.

"No more midnight rides with you," she sighed toward the black-clad figure.

"No more touches, no more kisses," he said.

Her chin quivered, her eyes grew misty. "I'm going to miss all the love, all the wonderful things we will never do," she said.

Her voice quavered. "I . . . I still can't believe it . . . you left me *alone*," she cried. "How . . . how can I make it alone?"

The sadness and strange aching made her feel weak. She was a fragile shell of herself, facing a bleak and sour future. Then he spoke to her.

"I love you. Remember that I love you," he said. "I'll always be close. Just close your eyes and think of our time together. We'll always have that, however brief . . . ."

"A jewel in time," she whispered. "A precious second . . . I won't forget . . . not ever."

"I held you in my arms," he said.

"And the world was all right again."

His voice was like a whisper. "That night, that moment . . . will always be."

He seemed to be fading.

No!

"Save that dream," he said. "Keep me in your heart . . . ."

"It . . . it hurts to say good-bye," she said, fighting back the tears.

"Our love will endure," he said, "even though we have to part." He touched her face. "Don't cry, Stephanie."

"Oh, it's so *unfair*," she complained, drifting away through the airbrushed reality. "I find you . . . and lose you . . . ."

"All that matters," he said, "is the time we had together, the *love* we had together."

"But—" Stephanie protested, feeling the thickening of harsh reality around her, "—I don't even know your name!"

His voice came to her as though from a great distance, from a time and place that maybe never was. "I love you," he said. "That's all you have to know . . . and that you are the only one who can remember our love and keep it alive." He smiled beneath his helmet's visor. "So . . . Stephanie . . . don't forget me . . . ."

Her hand went up, her heart went out. "I promise!"

The airbrushed world grew fainter.

"Remember," the rider said, "I love you . . . I'll always be close. . . ."

She hugged herself. "I can just close my

eyes," she whispered, "and it will all come back . . . ."

"All come back . . . ."

There was a thunder of applause that came over her like a wave, crashing about her, bursting through the airbrushed walls of Stephanie's grief. To her surprise, she found herself on her knees on the auditorium stage.

People were clapping and yelling.

Some were crying.

She stared around, blinking, surprised, and bewildered. *Was it a dream? What was it?*

She saw Michael Carrington in the wings looking at her, then turning away. She saw Miss McGee coming out, smiling, holding Nogerilli's arm.

The principal reached down and pulled Stephanie to her feet, holding both her arm and the arm of the swaggering Nogerilli. The Pink Ladies, the T-birds, and others crowded onto the stage to hear what was obvious to them all.

"The winners," Miss McGee announced, "of the talent show *and* king and queen of the last day of school's Lani Kiawani Luau!"

The applause was deafening, and Stephanie's tears began again. She felt weak and her knees started to give way. Nogerilli tore his arm from McGee's grasp and did a fighter's two-fisted victory gesture, but he took time to give Stephanie a searing, angry look.

Sharon gripped Stephanie's arms and supported her. "*Smile*, Stephanie."

"I mean," Paulette said over the din, "you won the whole talent show."

"*Girl's* division, Paulette," Sharon corrected.

"That's not so bad," Rhonda admitted.

But Dimucci couldn't believe it. "I can't believe it," he said. "We got half the records—all classical."

The applause continued.

And so did Stephanie's tears.

☆ CHAPTER 16 ☆

It was spring. "Lawrence of Arabia" was out. Sophia Loren, Maximilian Schell, and "West Side Story" had won Oscars. A couple of astronauts had been into orbit. Television was into repeats. "Sing Along With Mitch" was popular. Adolf Eichmann had been hanged in Israel. The Bank of Nova Scotia robbery in Montreal was one of the biggest ever. "Search for Tomorrow" was the big soap opera of weekday television. The New York Yankees looked good to take the series, "Lucy" was incredibly popular. Liston had taken the heavyweight title from Patterson. Some guy named Reynolds was hot with some of the girls in the reruns of "Dan Raven." A lot of guys were imitating Maynard the beatnik on "Dobie Gillis."

It was spring.

Students were putting the finishing touches on the luau decorations, moving the thatched huts and propping up palm trees, hanging signs and fixing costumes. Signs painted on cloth, RYDELL HIGH LUAU, ALOHA, hung over the entrances to the little huts where games were to be played. They were all in a big circle on one end of the main playing field.

A reed fence surrounded everything. In the center, a portable swimming pool had been set up, with steps leading to the four-foot-wide lip around it. Everything was draped with leis of plastic flowers, grass, and netting.

Nogerilli had his shirt off and was flexing his muscles, well aware of his giggling audience of freshmen and sophomores not far off. Paulette was sitting on the grass stringing together plastic flowers to make colorful leis. She frowned at him.

"What do you think you're doin', showin' them muscles like that?" she said heatedly.

"It's summer," he explained and shrugged. "I'm workin' on my tan."

"Yeah, well, you're gettin' overworked. No guy of mine shows that to nobody but _me_. Got it?"

"Got it, got it," he muttered and gave one more flex.

He flopped down on the grass, just a

touch sullen, under Paulette's watchful eye. She impulsively grabbed him. "Now come here!" She planted a big kiss right on his lips.

By the hut labeled "The Kissing Hut," Dolores stood with her back to Davey and the other student workers and stuffed wads of tissue into her bikini top. She acknowledged his fidgeting with, "One sec! One sec!" Then she turned, holding her hands out and thrusting her augmented chest forward. "Taa *daaa!* Instant sex!"

"Not bad," he said, trying to sound convinced of her sex appeal.

"Then I'm your grad date?" she asked eagerly.

"All right," Davey said, giving in. "All right. But don't make a big deal outta it."

She leaped on him and started kissing wherever her lips fell.

Sharon patted her Jackie Kennedy hairdo just once more, then spoke quietly but insistently to Dimucci. "You *have* to wear a dark blue suit," she said. "I don't want us to clash."

"*I'm* wearing my T-bird jacket," he said stubbornly.

Sharon whispered to him with more intensity. "If you want to get past second base, Louis, you'll wear a dark blue suit."

He let his eyelids droop.

Rhonda and Goose were struggling near the "Hut of Enchantment," with the T-bird trying to pin her down onto the grass in the shade. She was also very careful and protective of her nose, which, after all these many weeks, no longer sported a bandage.

"Watch the nose!" she snapped.

"How do we do it if I can't get within a mile of your beak?" he complained.

She was very firm. "First I get on 'National Bandstand.' Then it's your turn."

Goose groaned in frustration. He rolled over on his stomach and stared at the cheerleaders working out. Anything to keep from thinking about his weeks and months of total frustration. Goose took it all in without thinking about it. Hips swayed and legs kicked. Tops jiggled and bottoms bounced. Goose grinned. The third one from the left— the blondie with the bounce—she was the best of the new freshman crop.

Over at the side, Paulette, Sharon, Rhonda, and Dolores, wearing rather skimpy grass skirts, were dancing along with the cheerleaders and having a good time.

Some sorority girls passed by, their eyes sweeping over the Pink Ladies as if they were uncollected garbage. "It's girls like that who give summer fun a bad name," one said to the other.

But the Pink Ladies gave them the ultimate insult. They hadn't even paid any attention.

Stephanie sat alone in the stands, wearing dark glasses. She watched listlessly as Mr. Stuart helped Miss Mason into the rubber dinghy and they launched themselves precariously into the swimming pool.

Kids were fooling around, dancing and singing, playing carnival sideshow games at the huts, but none of it touched her. It was like watching a dumb movie with the sound off. She saw a rickshaw coming through the gate, carrying some teachers. A bunch of giggling girls ran up the steps and dived into the swimming pool to form a rather inept imitation of an Esther Williams aquacade around the rubber dinghy.

Mr. Stuart leaned toward Miss Mason in her flowered dress. "I've never told this to anyone before, Miss Mason," he began, nervously, but eagerly. "But I have this novel inside me just screaming to get out. I'd . . . I'd love to discuss it with you some evening."

Out came the can of hairspray, her hand whipping it around her head in a protective net. "Why, that's fascinating, Mister Stuart," she said, almost simpering.

"Call me Bud," he said.

"In that case," she said, carefully stowing the hairspray back in her purse. "In that case, Bud, there's something I've been *dying* to do all semester."

He was puzzled, and only his shyness prevented him from suggesting a few things. "What's that, uh, Yvette?"

She took off her glasses with deliberateness and stowed them in her voluminous purse, clinking against a spare care of spray. Then she leaned forward and reached out for him, planting a sudden and unexpected kiss on his startled lips.

"Eeeeee—!"

Over went to rubber dinghy and splash went the teachers.

It surprised no one that when Miss Mason surfaced, the water just ran off her hair, leaving it quite dry.

Blanche pulled a roast chicken from the picnic basket and inspected it. Roast chicken was something she did quite well, she thought. The secret was in the stuffing.

Coach Calhoun lifted up his starting gun behind her, checking the contestants in the three-legged race. He got the nod from Miss McGee and triggered the gun.

Pow!

The chicken exploded skyward, propelled by Blanche's surprised fingers. And Miss McGee caught it in her equally surprised hands.

Michael wound up and threw a ball with ferocious force—but not much accuracy—at the knock-down pineapples. The ball thumped off the canvas backing of the hut and Frenchy made a sound of commiseration.

"Forget it," Michael growled.

"If you say so," Frenchy agreed.

He turned and took a few stiff steps away. "I'm driving myself *crazy*," he said in a fierce whisper.

"If you say so," Frenchy said.

"Who needs her?" Michael snapped. "She's not worth it."

"If you say so," Frenchy said.

He looked at her angrily. "Well, what do *you* say?"

She shrugged and grinned. "*I* say it's the last day of school and you should give her one last shot."

Michael just stared at her. Then he looked at Stephanie, alone in the stands. He squared his shoulders. He swallowed. He hitched his belt. He squinted. "Okay," he said tightly, "I will."

There were a lot of students around the flower-decked pool, wearing Levi cutoffs, Hawaiian shirts, bikinis, trunks, flower leis, T-shirts, and tennis shoes.

There was a loud clearing of the throat, and the students saw that Coach Calhoun was on the podium, under the thatched grass roof. He held the microphone as if it were a deadly snake. "I'd like to say a few words about the meaning of the ancient Hawaiian ritual, the luau." He cleared his throat and the students shifted their feet. "Hundreds and hundreds of years ago," he began.

The sun went down right on schedule according to Blanche's almanac, and the torches were lit according to Miss McGee's schedule. And still Calhoun was saying his few words. "The luau guest danced and ate and ate and danced right into the night. They had to be in shape," he admitted. "Conditioning was everything way back then."

Miss McGee had had enough. More than enough. She took the microphone from Calhoun's hands and said brightly, "Thank you, Coach Calhoun. I'm certain that we are magnificently informed on the subject now, far more than we were this afternoon." She smiled brightly and some of the students— now sitting on the grass—applauded. They began to rise as Miss McGee continued. "Would the king and queen of the luau take their positions on the pool of enchantment?"

Blanche swung her big padded mallet at the gong from the music department, but instead hit the support for the podium roof.

The roof fell on both Blanche and McGee, and the gong made a strange rattling sound.

But that didn't stop the principal of Rydell High School. She scrambled for the fallen microphone and proudly announced the names. "From the senior class of 1961, Miss Stephanie Zinone and Mister John Nogerilli!"

"That is you, your holiness," Goose grinned and poked at Nogerilli.

"All right," he grunted.

They started off, Johnny in front, supported by the rest of the T-birds.

Paulette tugged at Stephanie's arm. "Come *on*! Ya *gotta* go!"

"This is a big deal," Sharon said.

"This is bigger than one person, Steph," Rhonda argued.

"This is bigger than *all* of us," Paulette said.

Stephanie breathed out and got to her feet. She was the only one of the escorting girls who was not smiling.

"Up!" Bruce Sanders commanded. The students, dressed in Hawaiian costumes, heaved the war canoe to their shoulders. Stephanie's eyes popped wide, and Nogerilli grabbed the sides of the fiberglass boat as they were lifted up.

"Hey!" he snapped.

The Hawaiian carriers dipped and buckled a bit, but they managed to get their cargo up the steps and launched into the pool, with much cheering by all.

Stephanie and Nogerilli faced each other, but sat stiffly, holding onto the edges of the craft, uncomfortable because of their sudden proximity, their status as objects of eager attention, and not least of all the fact they both might drown at any moment.

A noise came through the laughter and applause. It was the sound of motors and bikes.

Whap! Crash!

A motorcycle came thundering through one of the huts, carrying the remnants of the fence with it.

Six Cycle Lords roared onto the field. Three more followed. They tore through the middle of the luau, scattering students before their 600-pound metal monsters, toppling tables, knocking down fragile huts, dumping bowls of fruit, ripping down signs.

Nogerilli let out a cry of frustrated anguish and started paddling with his hands toward the edge. Stephanie, wide-eyed, helped. There was total chaos—screams, curses, yells, and crackling thumps.

☆CHAPTER 17☆

The Cycle Lords, grinning wolfishly, swung their bikes around and stood idling in a line at the end of the field. They surveyed the damage they had caused with smug satisfaction. Balmudo leered and swept his eyes across the littered grass—dinners made into instant garbage, screaming kids, deep ruts caused by the heavy machines.

Suddenly, he saw the black-clad figure standing arrogantly atop one of the last remaining huts.

"It's that loner!" Balmudo snarled. "That's the guy who decked me!"

Hands twisted grips. Engines roared. Wheels spun on green grass. With fierce cries, the Cycle Lords raced toward the figure on the hut.

Nogerilli jumped onto the deck of the

pool and turned toward where the Lords were charging. "Him!"

"Him!" exclaimed Sharon.

"*Him!*" Dolores said.

"Him?" Rhonda asked.

"Him," said Paulette.

Stephanie tore off her sunglasses and stared at the tall figure. She saw him leap off the hut and onto his bike. The machine roared, he did a wheelie to get through an obstruction, and then was off, thundering down the field.

The savage horde of the Cycle Lords was right behind him.

But the loner was not going toward the street. He had wanted to, but the way was blocked by a group of startled and frightened students. He swerved and clattered up the steps to Rydell itself, thumping through the doors and into the halls.

The cycle was deafening in the closed space, and when the Lords followed the leader the noise was beyond belief.

Michael skidded to a stop, leaned out, and pulled open the door of one of the classrooms. He kicked it open wider and drove his cycle right in.

Mr. Spears sat behind the desk, shaking, talking to himself. "The doctor is right. Of course, the doctor's right. The environment of the school is *much* healthier than the hospital."

Michael gunned across the room, hitting and scattering some of the seats in the last row, and smacked open the doors on the opposite side.

"Of course, it's healthier," Mr. Spears said, oblivious to the passage and equally oblivious to the rattling reverberation of nine more motorcycles transiting his classroom.

"Schools are places of learning," he said calmly and rationally. "Islands of peace, motels of calm in the turmoil of the world, refuges of sanity." He couldn't hear himself, but then he didn't need to.

"Hospitals are for sick people," he said. "Dying people. I'm not sick. I'm perfectly fine. Nothing wrong with me. I'll just sit here and teach. Class!" he said to the last departing Cycle Lord. "The subject today is stress in modern living. If you turn your textbooks to chapter five, you'll see how to cope with it. It's not important that I am also the author of this book, *Stress and Judgmental Coping in the Modern World*, what is important is that you pass the test."

Michael crashed through the exit doors, across a driveway, past a school bus, then swerved to miss a group of wide-eyed freshmen in Hawaiian shirts. That sent him back out toward the playing field. He quickly looked over his shoulder. The Cycle Lords were streaming out of the school behind him. He gunned it and raced toward the thatched village.

"Get 'im!" Balmudo screamed.

Close behind, they saw the loner zoom across the field and go right up the steps of the swimming pool!

If he can do it, we can do it, thought Balmudo, who didn't even slow down.

The lone rider was airborne, sailing magnificently across the pool, sitting straight and proud on his flying bike.

The Cycle Lords followed Balmudo blindly up the steps and into the air.

But the lone biker was the only one to clear the water and crash down on the steps on the other side, unscathed and untouched.

The splashdown was almost continuous as the Lords plunged into the pool.

The eighth one braked in time, but the last of the Lords bumped him coming up the steps, adding him and his machine to the depths of the pool. Water flowed out, splashing over the platform, and the ninth rider slipped as he started to turn his Harley and go back down.

Sploosh!

He and machine were baptized.

The crowd began running toward the

mystery biker as he braked to a stop beyond the pool. Dimucci and Davey pushed their way roughly through the thickening mob and reached the center just as Michael Carrington shoved up his dark visor.

"*You!*" Dimucci exclaimed.

Davey's mouth gaped open. "*You* made *that* jump?"

Stephanie pushed her way through the admiring crowd around the tall figure, coming up to Michael's back. "I thought you were—"

Michael turned and her blue eyes grew big, "—*You!*"

He shrugged shyly. "Yeah," he admitted.

Stephanie paused and rearranged reality in her mind. Then she flung herself around his neck. They kissed while those around them grinned happily.

"Awww . . ." a girl said.

"Outta my way," Nogerilli ordered, shoving roughly through the crowd. "Move it. C'mon, *move it!*" He got to the kissing couple just as they broke the kiss and he saw Michael's face looking at him from the lone rider's helmet. "You!"

"Hi, Johnny," Michael said casually.

Nogerilli shouldered Stephanie aside to grab Michael's jacket. "You got one more jump to make, hotshot. Over *me.*"

Stephanie shoved back between them.

"Stop!" she ordered. "Haven't we had *enough* of this?"

Davey Jaworski muttered, "She's got a point, Johnny."

"Davey's got a point, Johnny," Dimucci mumbled.

"Lou's got a point about Davey's point," Goose blurted.

Nogerilli's head turned toward them. "Shuuuud*up*, all o' you. I got a point to make, too." He released Michael's jacket to snap his fingers imperiously. "My jacket."

Davey quickly found it and gave it to the T-bird leader. "One T-bird jacket," he said.

Nogerilli took it and in one move handed it to Michael. "For starters, let's just see how it looks."

Dolores pushed her way through the crowd and up to Michael as he shrugged into the leather jacket. She jabbed him in the ribs and gestured for him to bend down. In Michael's ear, she said earnestly, "Listen, I don't think I can see you anymore. I'm sorta goin' with another man now."

Michael kissed her cheek. "It's too bad we didn't meet in another place at another time."

She shrugged philosophically. "That's the breaks."

Michael and Stephanie smiled at each other right into a long kiss. Paulette nudged

Nogerilli, who snapped out his hand. "Comb!" he commanded. Goose slipped it into his hand quickly. "About face!" Nogerilli ordered. Everyone turned with a grin and when Nogerilli called out "March!," they marched away.

Michael looked into Stephanie's eyes. "I never thought you'd kiss me like that if you knew who I really was."

"Are you crazy?" she smiled. "I get two for the price of one."

"You're certain?" asked the unmasked lone rider.

"I've never been certainer," she replied.

"More certain," he corrected.

"The *certainest*," she responded.

They just looked at each other for a long moment, savoring the seconds, memorizing them for all time.

"You were the one," Stephanie said, "the one in my dreams . . . but I never knew it."

"I . . . I wanted to tell you," Michael said, "time and again . . . but I couldn't do it."

She hugged him and said, "No more pretending."

"Now I can be *me*," he said. "And you can be you. And we're never ending." They kissed softly.

Nearby, Nogerilli gave Paulette a quick up-and-down look, then shrugged. "I like what you got," he said, very cool. "I . . . I guess it's okay, if you want to show it."

"I am what I am," Paulette said. "And I'm all for you . . . ."

"Will I ever score?" Dimucci asked Sharon, who shrugged and patted her Jackie Kennedy hairdo.

"Hey, there's nothing wrong with just likin' each other," she said and his face fell.

"We all had our doubts," Rhonda said.

"But it's workin' out," Goose admitted.

"We'll be together," Davey said.

"Always together," Dolores added, looking at Davey warmly.

"Like birds of a feather," Goose said, grinning.

"Forever and ever," Rhonda said. "We'll be together."

It was summer vacation. School was over. The future was ahead, where it should be. The world was for the taking. And they intended to take it.